ADVENTURES OF
THE RAMROD RIDER

Gripping Tales

Books by John D. Nesbitt

For the Norden Boys
Lonesome Range
Black Hat Butte
Red Wind Crossing
Rancho Alegre
Raven Springs
Coyote Trail
Black Diamond Rendezvous
Man from Wolf River
Not a Rustler
West of Rock River
North of Cheyenne
Poacher's Moon
Adventures of the Ramrod Rider
A Good Man to Have in Camp
Keep the Wind in Your Face
Shadows on the Plain
Field Work
Blue Horse Mesa: Western Stories
Antelope Sky: Stories of the Modern West
Seasons in the Fields: Stories of a Golden West

Two Novellas:
"Dead for the Last Time"
"Trouble in the Labor Camp"

ADVENTURES OF THE RAMROD RIDER

Gripping Tales

Augmented and Revised

By the Author

John D. Nesbitt

SPEAKING VOLUMES, LLC
NAPLES, FLORIDA
2017

ADVENTURES OF THE RAMROD RIDER

ISBN 978-1-62815-701-7

For my son, Dimitri,
buen compañero

Acknowledgments

"The Ramrod Rider Meets a Man of Wisdom" appeared in *Colorado State Review*, Spring-Summer 1984.

"Adventures of the Ramrod Rider, Price Ten Cents," "Further Adventures, Price the Same," and "Wyoming Welcomes the Ramrod Rider" appeared as a slim volume entitled *Adventures of the Ramrod Rider: A Trio of Gripping Tales* (1991).

"When My Pony Sheds Again" appeared on the website *readthewest.com*, September 1999.

The author is now pleased to set forth this fuller volume.

To the Reader

Do you yearn to wash your face in a mountain stream? Smell the aroma of woodsmoke? Taste of the simple fare that is cooked on a campfire? See the spread of the great Western sky above? Hear the click of a six-gun or the whinny of a horse?

Do you believe that fair maidens should be helped or that humble folk should be defended against the schemes of grasping overlords?

Would you like to ride the trail of adventure and danger, a trail that is as fresh and real now as it was a hundred years ago?

If you answered "yes" to any of the above, then turn the page and hold onto your hat.

Table of Contents

Adventures of the Ramrod Rider, Price Ten Cents

Death Comes for the Ramrod Rider

It was a dry and breathless summer afternoon on which a lone rider picked his slow and careful way down the western foothills of the mountain range between Nevada and Northern California. Horse and rider were one in a coat of trail dust, and they moved as inconspicuously as a deer. Utilizing all possible cover with great skill and care, the rider nudged his horse among the oaks and rocks. An observer would scarce notice the motion, for no shiny objects had been left exposed to the resilient rays of the sun. Presently the foothills sloped into a fertile and verdant valley, through the middle of which rippled the warm and placid Sacramento River.

But the river lay at a distance of several miles, and the rider, wishing to slake the thirst of both himself and his steed, made for a tributary brook that tumbled near at hand. There was a small clearing to cross, but there being no signs of hostile folk—no glint of rifle barrel, no rising trail dust, no column of smoke—he elected to cross the clearing rather than circumnavigate it. As horse and rider finally emerged from the oaks, the parching sunlight broke full upon the lean and haggard features of the man, bedecked in black, who called himself the Ramrod Rider.

Whence he came, and whither he went, were matters he broached with no man. It sufficed that he had come West, that he rode alone, and that he troubled no one. But the dull, smooth pistol grips, jutting out from the sheaths that were clasped to his thighs, would convey to the observer that here was a man whose life had not been without violence.

At present he wished for nothing more than a drink of water and a rest. He first let the horse drink in the purling brook, then bathed his own face, quenched his thirst, and filled his canteens. Next he mounted his buckskin stallion—for such it was—and directed it down the middle of the stream for perhaps a quarter mile. Then, emerging on the bank opposite the one from which he had embarked, he drew up on a grassy sward enclaved by willows and cottonwoods. Here he stripped his horse and picketed it to graze, then stretched himself in repose with his head on the saddle. After a short while, he reached into his saddlebags, withdrew a bundle of documents, and began to peruse them. Frequently he looked about him, ever vigilant for telltale movement or noise.

As he gave his attention to these papers, the contents of which no man was privy to beyond the Ramrod Rider, there emerged a second rider from the foothill oaks. This man showed no concern for his backtrail, but for the hieroglyphics of the first man's trail he showed the most sedulous scrutiny. Perceiving the direction of his quarry's trail across the meadow, he kept to cover around the edge of it. He saw where the rider went into the stream, and thus he divined the other man's motive. With a grimace of comprehension playing upon his unclean visage, he followed the stream from his side.

2

Before long, the hunted man's camp came into view, and the predator's first glimpse was of the Ramrod Rider tucking the papers into the saddlebags and arising from his repose. Now was no time to attack the enemy, for as the wary rider moved about to set his camp, his hands hovered always over the grips of his revolvers. With the patience of an Apache, the hunter drew away, knowing that with nightfall would come opportunity.

Came evening, and with it the smell of woodsmoke, broiled meat, and coffee. The pursuer bided his time, whittling a wooden effigy of the man he sought. When at length he thought the time had come, he lopped off the head of the miniature rider and put his knife in its sheath. Now picking up the agent of death, Monsieur Winchester, he stealthily crept to the knoll which he had chosen as his vantage point. From this spot he had a comprehensive view of the Ramrod Rider's camp; and there, illumined by the glowing embers of the campfire, the man saw a recumbent shape in a bedroll. Grinning with satisfaction, he raised his rifle, and with unerring aim and lightning-like rapidity, the ambassador of death pumped six Winchester slugs into the blanketed mound by the campfire.

The Ramrod Rider Makes an Acquaintance

This unexpected barrage of rifle fire would surely have been the death of the Ramrod Rider, had he not been in the bushes answering the exigencies of Dame Nature. For, sooth to say, he had imbibed a few cups of coffee, laced with the tonic which the rubicund tribesmen of the Plains called fire water. And so it was that he was surprised, but at a safe distance, by the outburst. Then through the horrid still of the night came the ululation of triumph, a sardonic laugh, and the retreating hoofbeats of a horse.

As the hoofbeats died away, the wary man eased forward the hammers of his six-guns, relaxed the poise of those two weapons, and slipped them into their holsters. At the first sound of gunfire, the guns had leapt into action, as if under their own power, so instantaneous and instinctive was the double draw of the Ramrod Rider.

Now the hunted man moved stealthily through the brush, circling the small clearing that held his camp. With both hands he eased the brush away from him, and his unshod feet sought out the quietest path. The moon was high and bright now, and its flooding glow lit up the sylvan stage across which the rider now crept. He was certain his attacker had ridden off, but he did not wish to loom as an easy target in such moonlight.

At length deciding that he was alone, he elected to finish his night's sleep. He gathered up his perforated bedroll and slipped into the surrounding cover, there to slumber lightly and inconspicuously under the auspices of a large manzanita.

The morning breeze wafted to his ears the sounds of the woods—birds, squirrels, chipmunks, and other small life that chirped of safety. The Ramrod Rider gathered up his bedding and cautiously made his way back toward his camp. As he reached the clearing, he saw the back of a man crouched at a small fire, apparently busy at breakfast. Dropping the bedroll and sliding both Colts from their holsters, he stepped out of the brush.

"Hold it right there, pardner," said he, punctuating his command with the double click of the pistol hammers.

The man at the fire turned to show a grizzled and bearded, but kindly, face. In his hands he held a handsome Bowie knife, which he had been in the act of employing to cut rashers of venison from a haunch he held on his left knee.

"No need for hardware, young man," said the stranger. "If this be your campfire I'm sharing, you're welcome to share my meat in return."

The Ramrod Rider, for whom the cervine cuts were second to no other, holstered his guns and came forward. "What makes you so free with another man's camp?" he asked.

The older man, now greasing the skillet with a scrap of bacon flitch, answered calmly. "I thought the camp was free to be used."

"How so?" queried the Rider, narrowly.

"I come down the foothills for water, like yourself. I seen the tracks of one man follerin' another, and then I heard a cluster of shots. Come mornin' I stumble onto a vacant camp, and, not wishin' to hurt yer feelin's, I figger the last feller hain't much use for it."

"Well," said the rider, "I still do have some use for it, as you can see. I'll rustle us up some coffee while you fry breakfast." Without further ceremony he made coffee, all the while fascinated by the older man's dexterity with the Bowie—cutting the slices, and then turning and manipulating them in the skillet.

When breakfast was over, the Ramrod Rider fished out the makings and rolled himself a cigarillo. He extended the pouch to the old man, who rolled a quirly with one hand while with the other he picked his teeth with the Bowie.

"Tell me," said the rider, exhaling his first breath of smoke, "who you are. By your looks I can tell you're a hunter and trapper."

"Well," said the greasy old-timer, "a hunter and trapper I am. I'm an old coon from the way-up creeks, and I been to see the critter. As for my name—my given name is William Wilberforce Waggens, but on account of my early days on the plains, men called me Buffalo. I go by that." The old man wiped the Bowie on the sleeve of his buckskin shirt. "And now, young man," he resumed, "tell me about yourself."

At this invitation, the rider launched into the following epyllion.

The Ramrod Rider's Story Told

I'm kinda shy, but since you asked
    I'll tell my story to you.
Some of it's strange and some of it's plain,
    But every word is true.

I'm a ramrod rider and Apache fighter
    And a straight-shootin' son of a gun.
I like to ride and I like to rope
    And I like to have my fun.

6

ADVENTURES OF THE RAMROD RIDER

Back in '78, in the Lone Star State,
    I started punchin' cattle,
Well I learned the ways of longhorn strays,
    And my schoolroom was the saddle.

We rounded 'em up and headed north
    In the spring of every year,
We had thunderstorms and prairie fires,
    And I learned the meaning of fear.

For seven years I rode for the brand
    Of the well-known Rollin' J,
Then the bottom fell out and the ranch went bust,
    And I drew my final pay.

With a lariat, six-gun, bedroll and horse
    And fifteen bucks to my name,
I hit the trail that I knew so well
    Across the land I helped to tame.

Now the grubline way don't make much pay,
    But it kept me warm and fed.
For breakin' broncs it was bacon and beans
    And a place to lay my head.

It was honest work, and I'd still be at it,
    Punchin' cows and toppin' broncs,
But I had it out with a bad hombre
    In one of them honky-tonks.

It was Amarillo in the August heat,
    When tempers flared up hot,
I was wettin' my whistle in the Silver Thistle
    When he put me on the spot.

"Hey, saddle tramp," his voice boomed out,
    "You're stinkin' up the place.
"If you got any guts you'll turn around
    "And look me in the face."

As I turned around he pulled his gun,
    And I clawed for my forty-four.
His shot went wide but mine was true,
    And he soaked the sawdust floor.

It was self-defense but they locked me up,
    And the word came to my cell—
They hadn't had a hangin' for over a month,
    And I didn't have a chance in hell.

Then a halfbreed kid named Apache Pete
    Broke me out of that run-down jail,
And back on my horse, without my gun,
    I followed him down the trail.

He tied my wrists to my saddle horn
    With a piece of raw whipcord.
Then he laughed as he told me I'd be worth

ADVENTURES OF THE RAMROD RIDER

A thousand-dollar reward.

He spit in my face and took my reins,
    Then galloped ahead of me.
But as we rode in the moonlit night,
    I worked the rawhide free!

In the ghostly pale of a desert night
    I strangled Apache Pete.
I took his rifle and full canteen
    And left him for buzzard meat.

Now the outlaw trail was mine to ride,
    Where water was hard to find,
With hidden camps and careful fires,
    And always a glance behind.

Across the badlands I rode west,
    Alone, by night when I could,
Till I came to the scent of mountain pine,
    Where the town of Santa Fe stood.

I rested there and watered well,
    Then west again I rode,
Farther from the crime I didn't commit,
    Farther down an unknown road.

    [Here the Ramrod Rider cleared his throat,
    in preparation for a change in meter.]

While in New Mexico I stayed for a spell
With a young bandit king whose name you know well.
This young outlaw monarch lived back in a cave,
Were in flickering torchlight close by him would wave
Dark-haired señoritas serving brandy and wine,
While out on the desert the coyotes would whine.
One night when the sun had gone down in the west,
As the regular feasting and drinking progressed . . .

The Ramrod Rider Takes a Ride

"Whoa, young man," interrupted Buffalo, as he ran his thumb along the Bowie blade in the rosy morning light. "If all you say is true, you done a heap of livin'!"

"You've just heard the start of it," said the rider, showing no sign of fatigue from the exercise of narration and its accompanying gesticulations.

"And you may both have heard the end of it," said a gravelly voice from the bushes. The duo at the campfire heard the ominous click of a pistol hammer, and they turned to look full upon a scarred face, bewhiskered and begrimed from the rugged trail life.

"What do you mean?" asked the rider, searching for a lapse in the other man's attention.

"I thought I took care of you last night, but I came back to make sure. Now I see I have twice the work to do."

"What grudge have you got against me? Who are you?"

The gunman smiled with leisurely malice. "I've gone by a dozen names and been called others," he sneered, "but I'm chiefly known from here to Robber's Roost as Durango Dan."

Durango Dan! The name rang like a shod hoof on *malpaís*. This was the ruffian who, years ago, had been brought to justice by the Ramrod Rider himself when the latter rode for the Rolling J. But time and an incessant residence in the lower purlieus of life had made the brigand's face harsher than ever, and thus unrecognizable. Now, as the famed cutthroat held them at gunpoint, the Ramrod Rider recalled that Durango Dan had broken prison and had sworn vengeance on the man who had sent him there.

"You're gonna shoot me in cold blood?" asked the rider.

"No," said the blackguard, grinning iniquitously. "I'm givin' you a fair chance this time." Ever holding the revolver leveled at the rider, Dan reached for his lasso, and with a rustler's agility he left-handedly dropped a loop over the head of the Ramrod Rider and snugged it. Deftly he wound three dallies around his saddle horn. Then, producing some rawhide thongs, he ordered Buffalo Waggens to bind the rider's wrists together in back and to hand the pair of pistols to the outlaw. These he secured in his saddlebags. Next he ordered Waggens to lie face down by the campfire. Durango Dan stepped into the saddle, gave his lead rope a slight tug, and headed his horse toward the mountains. As he lightly touched the spurs to the horse, he brought into compliance, like a maverick calf, the encumbered Ramrod Rider.

After an hour of arduous walking, the captive perceived that they were getting into rocky terrain. Huge boulders, upthrusts of granite, and jutting crags lined the trail up which Durango Dan brought them. At one juncture, the Ramrod Rider turned to look back down on the valley, but a peremptory jerk from the lead rope caused him to resume his peregrination. Presently the outlaw directed his mount into an aperture in the rocks, an entry-way which led into a narrow and tortuous defile of shadowy content. Twice the captive was jostled into the protruding walls, but still he kept his pace. To fall at this point might mean catastrophe or severe injury, and the Ramrod Rider had not yet given up hope of escape.

Now the passage-way opened onto the other side of the ridge they had just climbed, and one could see that a huge canyon lay before them. The outlaw turned right and conducted them along a rather wide ledge, a pathway that seemed to have had much use in years past. After some meandering along this path, Durango Dan brought them to a pause before a cave. A cavernous black mouth yawned at them; and like a serpent's tongue, a small railway led out of the grotto and turned down the path ahead of the travelers. The Ramrod Rider divined that this was an old mining shaft, and that the small track had been the route of conveyance for carts of ore.

Without a word, the swarthy ruffian dismounted and went into the cave, leaving his captive to stand on the brink of the sublime canyon and to ruminate on what this bravo might have in store. Many possibilities had as yet presented themselves to the imaginative faculties of the Ramrod Rider, but he was caught entirely by surprise at the sight that emerged from the cave. Into the sunlight from the ominous gullet there hove into view a rusty cart, a trolley wagon, behind which Durango Dan labored mildly.

"Get in!" he commanded, and with some ado the handicapped cowboy did so. "Here's your fair chance," growled the bully, removing the lead rope; "I won't tie you to the cart itself."

With a malignant snicker the outlaw gave the mining cart a shove, and after a few yards it began a downhill course. The Ramrod Rider, lashed as he was by the wrists, could barely elevate himself to see over the rim. Then, as the track followed a steeper declivity and the cart began to pick up speed, the rider looked out and saw that in about two hundred yards the track approached a curve. And there, where the track swerved out around the mountain, erosion had cut away the bank. The tracks ended in mid-air, and beyond them lay a deep and rocky gorge, a chasm from which, in view of the inevitable descent, no man could escape.

Farewell to the Ramrod Rider

Shortly after the departure of Durango Dan and the hapless Ramrod Rider, the worthy woodsman and plainsman Buffalo Waggens arose from his prone position by the campfire. On first impulse he took up his trusty muzzle-loading rifle, thinking to put a ball of lead between the outlaw's shoulder blades. But this plan he eschewed with the thought that the gunfire might spook the horse and thereby bring grief to his young friend's neck. And so the sagacious scout embarked upon a more subtle mission of rescue, taking to the rocks and warily following the pair ahead. When he saw them enter the passage through the rocks, he directed himself up and over the rimrock, hoping to keep the duo in his sight.

On the other side he saw nothing but the stupendous canyon . . . then he saw the roadway down below. He thought to himself that the path might lead him, either in pursuit or face to face, to his quarry.

When he had descended to the road, he began slowly and quietly to follow the tracks uphill. After half a mile, he came to a place where the road and the trolley track were washed out, at a corner beyond which he could not see. As he was pondering his impasse, he heard the rumble of what seemed to be an approaching cart. Then he saw a mining cart careen off the track and plummet over the edge of the precipice, a sight that was attended by the cascading crash of the cart down the canyon. He asked himself, had there been a passenger in that vehicle? Cautiously he crept to the edge of the cliff.

As the mossy visage of Buffalo peered over the rim of the canyon, it showed the greatest surprise at seeing, suspended by the arms from a jutting oak, the lithe and supple form of the Ramrod Rider. There had indeed been a passenger, and in the cart's headlong plunge he had apparently leapt free and grabbed hold of the gnarly oak. Now it remained for Buffalo to help bring the rider back to terra firma.

This he did, first by crawling out onto the oak and slashing the rawhide thong with his trusty Bowie, and then by extending a hand to bring the Ramrod Rider onto the trunk of the oak and thence up the shaly slide to the ledge. There they were safe, for they both knew that Durango Dan could not negotiate the eroded corner. Here they might rest, and regroup their forces.

"Well, young man," said the grizzled scout, "that there was a close brush with death."

"Sure was," replied the rider. "I was lucky I had time to get my hands in front of me where I could use them."

"Say," said the venerable plainsman, "what does this here Durango Dan have a-gin you in the way of a grudge?"

"Well," said the rider, drawing a deep breath as he had done before his last narration, "when I was the ramrod rider for the Rolling J, I helped convict this ruthless outlaw and send him to prison for stealing cattle. But he broke prison some years ago, cutting the throats of two guards, and he swore to get even with me. Now at last he has found me."

"That the long and the short of it?"

"Maybe not. I suspect he also plans to steal a mining claim I have in my saddlebags. It was given me by a generous man whom I saved from lynching, a man who later made a fortune in a secret mine here in the gold country. Fearful of the greed and violence of this West, he returned to the East. But in his wealth and leisure he remembered me, the Ramrod Rider, who had saved his life from an unjust fate. In his will he left me the mine, and that is what brings me west. Otherwise I might have stayed in New Mexico or Arizona, a hot and dry land where I am at home. Why, even as I left Santa Fe—"

At this point Buffalo cut in. "We better start makin' our plans. That feller won't give up easy."

"You got any ideas?" queried the rider.

"Got one that's perkin' a mite."

"Go on."

"Yer man Durango Dan won't be comin' 'round that corner," said Buffalo, pointing with his Bowie.

"No . . ." agreed the rider.

"An' he won't come droppin' over on us thisaway," he added, pointing to the granite escarpment under which they now sat.

"No . . ." repeated the cowboy.

"Then he'll be comin' around on us, on his way back to yer saddlebags."

"I think you're on the right trail," assented the Ramrod Rider, with marked enthusiasm.

"So I think we oughta get to the rimrock first, and get the drop on him."

"Partner, I'm glad you're on my side." The Ramrod Rider clasped the older man's hand in solidarity, then followed him up the mountainside.

Once up on the rim, the cautious pair were as silent as the surrounding rocks. The older man placed them by a trail which, through his previous reconnaissance, he esteemed would be the return route of Durango Dan. By and by the scuffing and jingling of spurred boots on rimrock alerted them that the moment of the encounter was nigh. The Ramrod Rider, perched on a rock above the trail, held his breath until the dusty sombrero of the outlaw loomed into view below him. Then he leaped.

Once the burly outlaw was in the grips of the Ramrod Rider, he fought like a crazed wild animal. The rider was obliged to call upon rare reserves of strength as the two men grappled, muscles taut as braided rawhide. At one juncture the outlaw settled both hands upon the throat of his adversary, and would surely have dashed his brains upon a rock, had the quick-witted rider not dexterously tripped the brute. Now they struggled again, rolling and scrambling, punching and thrusting, until they came to a deadlock at the peak of a promontory. Here the cliff fell away sharply, straight down to the place where the mining track had suspended itself in mid-air, and from there to the yawning vault of the canyon below.

Ambition flared in the eyes of the outlaw as he saw his enemy, jaw set in determination, backed up to the edge of the precipice. He instinctively reached for his whittling knife, only to find that it had fallen out in the preliminary phase of their struggle. Then his eyes lit upon a boulder, big as a man's head, as a likely weapon. Stealthily he crouched, picked it up, and raised it above his head. With a titanic effort he heaved the rock directly at the other, who stood silhouetted against empty space.

The Ramrod Rider all this while watched the eyes of his aggressor, and as the rock came up it blocked the outlaw's vision. Nimbly the rider stepped aside and ducked; as the rock flew into space, the rider grasped the right wrist of Durango Dan. Utilizing the heavy man's forward motion, he jerked him toward the cliff and released him. An unearthly howl of agony reverberated through the canyon as Durango Dan reaped the reward of his final deed. When the Ramrod Rider brought himself into position to see over the ledge, he saw only the mining track quivering in mid-air.

Back in camp, the Ramrod Rider saddled his horse, after first checking his saddlebags. He led the horse to drink at the rill that tumbled by as pleasantly as before. After shaking hands in wordless farewell with Buffalo Waggens, he stepped into the saddle and slung his leg over. He tipped his hat and reined the horse around. As the rider urged the horse into the broad and sunny trail, he knew that the trail would cross with other trails, some dark and sinewy, and that down one of those trails might lurk ambush, danger, and even death for the Ramrod Rider.

Further Adventures, Price the Same

The Ramrod Rider Meets a Man of Wisdom

One warm August afternoon many years ago, on the western slope of the Sierra Nevada, a lone rider and horse picked their tortuous way through boulders, oaks, and pines. The rider headed his horse for a jutting promontory of granite, which he hoped to gain for the purpose of scanning his backtrail. When finally the pair emerged from the trees, the sun shone full upon the man, bedecked in black, who called himself the Ramrod Rider.

As they crested the out-thrust of rock, the man was surprised to see a gaping cavern in the side of the mountain. Drawing closer, the rider could see that the grotto was inhabited and that its walls were lined with shelves sagging with dusty books and numerous sheaves of paper. Just as he was recovering from his surprise at this unlikely discovery, he saw an elderly but hale man emerge from the interior of the cave.

The man bore a look of profound gravity and serenity, and he walked with the tread of one who has traveled much in the woes and secrets of this life. His hands, as tenacious as talons, carried a large stack of parched and curled documents. His brows were thoughtful, thick and dark, and his hair had the venerable cast of silver. Upon seeing his visitor, he set his papers on a table and beckoned. Then he said, "Light and set."

The rider did so, taking his place on a boulder. The older man looked him over, and played at length with the Indian amulets that hung on his chest from around his neck. "Who are you?" he asked.

"Call me the Ramrod Rider," answered his visitor; "that's what I am."

"Call me Tex Barnes," said the cave-dweller, holding his hand up with the palm out.

"You live here?"

"This is my study, where I do my work. I write."

"What do you write?"

"My best-known works are the stories about the Baggett family—men of good horse, and fierce fighting men! Perhaps you have read *Barnabas Baggett and the Rustlers of West Fork, or Barnabas Baggett and the Riders of High Rock.*"

"Can't say that I have, but I've seen 'em. They sell like porkpie hats down in the settlements. Is the name Barnabas any kin to yer name, Mister Barnes?"

"My real name," said the *romancier* in a lowered voice, "is Luther Lambert, but years ago the name Tex Barnes presented itself as more poetical. But, yes, idle scholars have made much of my *nom de plume* and its kinship with my characters."

"Say," said the Ramrod Rider, "do you write them stories about Deadwood Dick and Solid Sam, too?"

Barnes took a deep and serious breath. "I am not a dime novelist," he said quietly, "no, nor a nickel novelist, though many consider me to be both. I am a weaver of tales." Then, catching the uncertain look of the Ramrod Rider, who himself had woven *reatas* of other parts of the bovine species, he promptly clarified. "A story teller. Beneath every work of beauty there is a framework, and over the centuries certain systems have been discovered that enable one to tell a story well. Such systems lie at the heart of Shakespeare and the poems of Homer . . . "

The Ramrod Rider interrupted at this point. Of Shakespeare he had heard, on account of his having written a story about a ham omelet, or something such. From the author's name, the worthy rider had assumed him to be a Plains Indian, and had been surprised to learn that he was a civilized white man. Of the second name, however, the rider was uncertain. "This here Homer—he a Nigro cowpuncher with a gold tooth? Sing lotta songs?"

The older man shot him a look that pierced like a Sioux arrow, and he continued by repeating the names of Shakespeare and Homer, then following with a catalog of names that were of foreign and mystical import, but that no wise struck a chord of familiarity with the unlettered Ramrod Rider. At the end of this chant of names, the learned man concluded by observing, "We who write stories understand that there are only a handful of situations upon which stories can turn, and it is the final measure of the man if he but write well. And even if a man write trash, it may be worth reading, for it is the product of much selection."

The rider, hoping to show interest, asked, "When you write about these Baggett fellows, I reckon you write about Injuns?"

"I have enormous respect for my craft and one of the first things one learns is to ascertain the facts. Yes. I have spent many nights and days in the wigwams and wickiups of the Ute, the Crow, the Arapaho, the Mescalero . . . " The Ramrod Rider raised his brows. " . . . but I am *not*," emphasized his interlocutor, "a squaw man, though by your look you seem to think so."

"Lord, no," said the rider in awe, "I was just surprised you'd been around so much."

"The places I have been," said the venerable story-teller, "would raise your hair. For I have travelled the rivers west, ridden down the long hills, through the dark canyon and across the burning hills to where the long grass blows. I know what it is to ride the dark trail, whether it be under the Sweet-water Rim, up on the high lonesome, over on the dry side, or to the far blue mountains. Mine has been the proving trail, a crossfire trail, through all of Baggett's Land. And I have seen the tall stranger."

"You have seen much," said the rider, entranced.

"When I write about a spring, that spring is there, and the water is good to drink." The man of wisdom made a definitive flourish of the arm.

At this pronouncement, the Ramrod Rider cast a glance toward his own canteen, slung over the pommel of his saddle. "Speakin' of which," he said, "I'd like to cut the dust in my throat." Without further formality, he strode to his horse and produced the canteen in offering to the bard of Baggetts. The latter declined with stoic firmness, and the Ramrod Rider slaked his thirst without ado. Then, wiping the trail dust from his moistened mouth, he introduced the subject of victuals. "I got some hardtack and jerky here," he announced. " 'Bout time for a bite?"

The spinner of yarns nodded with Spartan solemnity. "Yes," he said, "and I can offer parched corn. And coffee." Then, as his eyes searched deep into the soul of the Ramrod Rider, he said, "It is strange. The Apache does not eat fish, nor pork. It is mule meat and horse meat he likes best. And he will not attack at night, for fear that his soul will wander forever in darkness."

After a quick check from the edge of the rock, whence he studied the country, the craftsman gathered dry fallen pieces from the curl-leaf, a shrub of which the branches give off a hot flame and are almost smokeless. He took care to build the fire beneath a large mesquite so that the smoke, what little there was, would be dissipated through the foliage. Thus there would be no rising column of smoke, no finger beckoning to hostile eyes. It was a small fire, a careful fire, and over it he made coffee and boiled the corn.

"A man must be careful of fires," he said, "even in good times."

They then ate in silence, as is often the way with men of the high trail. As the *raconteur* leaned to one side to set down his tin plate and cup, he lifted his haunch; wordlessly and with the decorum of a Cherokee chieftain, he expressed his satiety. Then, with vertical and horizontal slices of the hand, he pronounced, "Ven-ny-kat-na-wen-nee."

"Meanin?" queried the guest.

"Fair blows the wind."

The Ramrod Rider finished his coffee, shook out the grounds into the fire, and made ready to mount his steed. The savant stood, and he lifted his arm to the brassy sky above. He uttered two or three more Indian slogans, none of which signified clear meaning to the rider. Then the old man concluded their intercourse with saying, "It is good. There should be little said at time of parting."

He turned and directed himself again to his study and his multitudinous volumes and gatherings of documents. The Ramrod Rider sought out the trail, leaving the venerable Tex Barnes, who, in sedulous and reverent search of historical truth, resumed his indefatigable perusal of wine lists, bills of lading, and account-books of sundry Indian agents.

A Chance Discovery

Having partaken of the viands and of the aesthetics of the estimable chronicler, the Ramrod Rider now directed his steed toward Los Peñascos, a small growth on the lower toe of the Sierra foothills. Here he planned (provided that the wheel of fortune did not stop in the meantime) to take on provisions against the gruelling trek across the Mojave—for, dreaded though the Mojave be for its extreme heat and aridity, its paucity of refreshment for man and beast, and its plethora of the ubiquitous rattler, tarantula, and vinegaroon, it was across this merciless expanse that the rider's travels now took him.

Descending, then, from the slopes of piñon and juniper to the less auspicious flats of Joshua tree, sahuaro, and prickly pear, the Ramrod Rider bethought himself of the virtuous curl-leaf and of the eternal verity that patience is the price of survival in this indifferent and sometimes hostile zone.

A stranger to this particular locality but familiar with it through campfire palaver with other peregrinators such as himself, the Ramrod Rider elected to ride south by southeast through a flank of foothills he had descried from the higher elevations. Upon cresting one of several low ridges that lay in his route, and ever diligent to keep from skylining himself, the rider drew rein in the shadow of an imposing boulder, whence he scanned his backtrail, without cause for alarm, and whence he surveyed the land before him.

Below him the land sloped away on all sides to a small tableau in the center, so that the broader features of the landscape lent it a general resemblance to a dun and dusty tureen, empty save a small dollop of white in the bottom. Squinting his eyes against the rays of the sun and the heat waves of the landscape, the rider perceived that the whiteness was an excrescence and not a stain on the valley floor, and that it exhibited a remarkable propinquity, at this distance, to an encirclement of covered wagons.

With his heart gladdened at the prospect of an evening's society, the equestrian had as his first impulse the desire to descend in full view down the slope, to halloo the camp, and to break bread with his fellow man. This impulse, however, he checked, still affected as he was by the gravity and reserve of Tex Barnes, and by the vigilance conveyed to him by that personage. And so, upon a second and well-considered thought, he picked his way slowly down the declivity, utilizing all rocks, shrubs, gullies, and other natural obstacles to his best possible advantage.

Within a quarter mile's proximity of the enclave of wagons, the Ramrod Rider availed himself of an assembly of boulders, wherein he ensconced himself and his steed. Peering out through a cleft in the rocks, he studied the encampment; he soon saw, moving and browsing about, several horned and bearded specimens of the caprine race. "Goats," he breathed to himself—for he was not a man to mince words. Thinking he had happened upon a group of pastoral nomads, but yet ever cautious of unknown trails, the rider studied closer. Soon there were seen to ambulate about, in and among the flock, creatures of an ursine cast—dark brown, walking sometimes on two feet and sometimes on four, and repeatedly shrouded from view by the wagons.

His curiosity thus piqued, the wary rider chose to settle back in the shade of the rocks, there to while away the few remaining hours until dusk, under the aegis of which he would make a closer reconnaissance.

Came dusk, and with it the plaintive call of the desert quail, which told him that there was water near at hand, perhaps a spring or seep-hole, from which the flock of goats and its unspecified attendants might drink. The rider now bestirred himself, imbued though he was with lassitude; he secured his jingling silver-rowelled spurs in his saddlebag, adjusted the loosened cinch-girth on his horse, checked his revolvers, and moved stealthily out of his cover and into the thickening evening. Presently he came to a point from which he could see the camp.

Within the enclave, all was still. The shaggy race was upon its four knees, ruminating perhaps in both senses of the word, but certainly in the primary; the aboriginal tenders had withdrawn to as yet undisclosed quarters; and a campfire flickered on the far side of the enclosure. In the lambent glow there could be discerned three definite and discrete human forms—one holding forth as if lecturing, and two seated in attendance.

For a measured time, the rider bent his gaze upon this trio, regarded in detail their immediate environs, and, emboldened by his quest for knowledge, began a circumnavigation to a point from which he might overhear their talk. As the rider-turned-scout passed one wagon, however, he heard a commotion within, and an attending creak of the wagon frame. Capitulating to irresistible temptation, he drew back the flap of the wagon sheet. Instantly his nostrils were assailed by an indelicate and inhuman odor, the ammoniac stench of animal sweat and ordure. Within this wagon, as he now supposed could be found within several of the other vehicles, was situated a large bamboo cage which housed four hairy creatures—creatures which, upon this closer inspection, proved to be not ursine but simian.

As if muttering a bitter oath, the surprised rider pronounced, in a forced but stifled breath as he endeavored to master his incredulity, "Monkeys!"

Discoveries of a Deeper Dye

Under the impact of this redolent and unlikely disclosure, the Ramrod Rider moved on, hoping to add to his new but bewildering knowledge, this incipient knowledge now rife with mystery. Presently he was downwind of the assembled trio, and the breeze wafted their words to him.

"Here, Lunn-wahr, have some beans. You best take on some grub." The speaker was a thick-set, loutish sort, hunkered over a pot suspended from a tripod, and handing a tin plate to the standing man. The latter, from this distance, by virtue of his sartorial fastidiousness and his imperial posture, shone forth as clearly the leader of this band and of whoever else might be of their number.

"I *hate* beans," said the master, as he took an upward cut with his riding crop, and sent the plate twanging and beans flying. "Have we no food edible? I have several times told you that Le Noir Faineant" (and this he trilled with a tongue unmistakably French) "eats no beans. 'French' Louis!" This he pronounced with a note of disdain that conveyed to their unknown auditor that French "Looie" was of French extraction perhaps, but not of French nativity.

"Yup." Thus French Looie.

"Have we no comestibles? No *escargots*? No *cotelette de veau*?"

"Considerin' we poached that calf off the Double Ell this mornin', I reckon we got some veal cutlet, but I thought we might let 'er hang a day or so."

"I will not eat beans," enunciated Le Noir, tapping his crop in his left hand, in symphonic accompaniment.

"Rustle you up some in two shakes," said Looie, who pushed himself up and in the direction of what the Ramrod Rider now identified as the chuck wagon.

For the next fifteen minutes, there was no dialogue, and the breeze wafted only the savory and fragrant wisps emanating from the broiled veal. Now Le Noir Faineant was seated, not unregally, upon an unfolded chair, and was applying his sterling cutlery, brought forth in a leathern case from within his surtout, upon the meat.

"Got 'er cooked all right?" asked Looie, who had executed the cuisine and who was no doubt solicitous of pleasing his superior.

"You are becoming less barbaric," replied the chieftain, now tossing the remains into the fire.

"Hey," retorted French Looie, singularly unappreciative of the encomium bestowed upon him, "that's good meat yer tossin' out."

"Let them eat beans," returned Le Noir, accepting a glass of wine from his other lackey, who, it seemed, also assumed the station of wine steward, to the extent that he announced the wine as "some of that there claret." Le Noir nodded and said, "Thank you, Grubb."

Grubb! The Ramrod Rider now saw that Le Noir's lackey was none other than Emmett Grubb, that petty but inveterate thug besought by the myrmidons of justice from Tombstone to Laredo. And now, as the firelight played upon Grubb's face, his still undiscovered observer recognized the distorted visage that had looked upon a dozen jailers and twice as many victims. His crimes had been of the lowest order—livestock larceny, barn burning, well poisoning, and the like—most often suborned for the profit of those more powerful ruffians under whose favor he grovelled. This blackguard, now Le Noir's underling, had earned the kicks and rebuffs of every race on the frontier. He was a man to whom a spit in the face was as normal as a tip of the hat; furthermore, he was a man who lived for but three purposes: to convey whiskey and beans to his weasand, to curry the favor and draw upon the power of such desperadoes as Le Noir Faineant, and insidiously, with the most furtive duplicity, to revenge himself upon mankind for helping him become the wretch he now was.

"Explain to us how this is all gonna work, boss," Looie implored gently.

"You need not know more than your own duties."

"Aw, c'mon, Lunn-wahr," said Grubb, offering to pour more wine, "we know you've got a Jim-dandy scheme, and we'd be tickled to know what we're up to. There's just the three of us. It'll go no farther than this campfire." With that he threw a chunk of mesquite upon the fire, a chunk that proved to be green as it sent off billows of smoke that were wafted into the face of the hapless Ramrod Rider. With burning nostrils and stinging eyes he held firm, however, to listen forth, so strong was his devotion to truth and justice.

Le Noir took a second sip; then, perhaps eloquented by the grape, perhaps soothed by the flattery of his subordinates, or perhaps both, he acquiesced. As he did so, his observer, by the grace of a temporary shift in wind that fanned the flames, caught a full illumined view of the speaker.

The sybaritic Le Noir Faineant, as he stood bedecked in sable silks and satins, was without doubt alien to the bounteous West in both nationality and spirit. To the sagacious scrutiny of the Ramrod Rider, he was a man impervious to the beauties and the exigencies of this panoramic and rejuvenating region. Le Noir's eyes were but slits of malice through which cupidity peeked out for opportunity. Thinly wreathed around teeth not unlike those of the weasel were two dry and bloodless lips, the upper of which sported a thin mustache that might have been pencilled in by the grand artificer of fraud himself. With histrionic deportment he brandished aloft his riding crop, and with a petite flourish of that implement, he commenced his explication.

"This land, as you know, has no value," he began.

"Well, now, Le Noir, any piece of land is liable to be worth somethin'," interposed French Looie.

"Do I continue?" inquired Le Noir, raising his eyebrows.

"Sure, go ahead. Sorry."

"Very well. This land, as you know, has no value. It is owned variously by the government and by stupid, yes, stupid, American men of affairs who have hoped to find mineral wealth here. That in itself is ridiculous, but fortunate for my aspirations." Here a sip on the claret. "This valley, as it is called, is the property of the government. That line of hills is owned by one investment company, and that other line of hills is owned by another group of, shall we say, not very intelligent investors?" Another sip.

"Sure. We know that." Grubb decanted more wine.

"Both ridges are for sale, with the stipulation that the same party does not buy both, for fear that the government land will be under the control of the surrounding party." Here Le Noir laughed, more to himself than to his audience. "At the end of this valley there is, elevated somewhat, many caves which were in years past inhabited by your savages. It is those caves, and all access and egress, which I hope to control."

"What truck you got with them caves?" inquired Grubb, bluntly.

"I have designs, which may exceed your comprehension, but I will continue. You, Grubb, will purchase land on one side of this valley, and you, 'French' Looie, will purchase the land on the other side. You will each pretend to think that there is silver or copper in the land, and by your looks, they will remark that you quite probably are so . . . thick-headed as to think so."

"You mean we buy the land, with your money?"

"Exactly. And with the land secure, I may proceed to use the caves for my science."

"Your science?" French Looie looked askance.

"Precisely. I hope to, shall we say, experiment with some of these monkeys."

"Then we don't have to do any more trainin' of these monkeys, to teach 'em to ride these consarned goats?" Grubb sounded hopeful.

"Their training will continue, but under the instruction of new trainers. Tomorrow there will arrive four little men about this tall; how do you call them?"

"Midgets?" queried French Looie.

"That is it. Midgets. They will train the monkeys and goats, and we will have a *petite* Wild West Show, a perfect cover for my experiments. It is a wonderful American enterprise, no?" Le Noir sipped yet again on the claret, his mirth clearly remontant.

"I didn't think you were all that stuck on cowboys," postulated the lackey, Grubb.

"I *hate* cowboys!" enunciated Le Noir, emphasizing with his inflection that he was as inimical to the sons of the sagebrush as he was to beans. "But the little midgets will also help me in the evenings with my experiments. Their cowboy clothes will be, as I have said, a disguise. They are well-trained scientists."

French Looie now made manifest the truth that he was superior in intellect and diplomacy to his colleague, Grubb. "If you don't mind, Le Noir, could you tell us a little about those experiments? If we knew a little bit, we might be able to head off trouble when it comes peekin' and pokin' around."

"Very well," complied the Frenchman. "It is a science only in the American sense—that is to say, it is a business of profiting from the discoveries of science. You have seen in the cities, perhaps, such things as museums and circuses?"

"You betcha," Grubb responded, readily.

"I was certain you had had such illumination," sneered Le Noir. "In those displays, perhaps you have seen such curiosities as 'mummies'?"

"Those Egyptians that have been dead for hundreds of years?" inquired French Looie.

"The same. Well, to be brief, the climate in this region, barbaric perhaps, is perfect—let me repeat, perfect—for the desiccation of these monkeys into a state of verisimilitude to mummies." Here he sipped on the claret, paused theatrically, and resumed. "And the Americans will buy them! They buy them for thousands of dollars apiece! Ha! Ha! Ha! Ha! I am a marvelous American, am I not?"

The Ramrod Rider Seeks Counsel

It would indeed be difficult to exaggerate the surprise of the Ramrod Rider at this juncture. Here was a plot to encroach upon government land, to defile ancient cliff dwellings, and to exploit the simian race—all to line the coffers of the miscreant Le Noir. Stunned and nearly prostrated by this newly gathered intelligence, the rider sat awhile in silence. Then it occurred to him that the wagon under which he had thus long been obscured had not given forth any sign of inhabitants. Knowing that it was not the chuck wagon, the rider considered that this wagon might lend some further clue to the web of perplexing circumstances he was now apprehending. Slipping cautiously, ever so cautiously, to the rear of the wagon, with a wary eye toward the three men at the campfire, he parted asunder the flaps of the wagon. His eyes, already accustomed to the murky darkness, quickly took in several crates of what seemed to be elixir, for all the crates were identical, and one was opened. From this open crate, he drew forth a bottle, and then he made his escape.

Back in the shelter of rocks, he opened the bottle and smelled of it. It was certainly not liquor, but some other foreign substance, some chemical no doubt manufactured for unnatural purposes—but for which purposes, the Ramrod Rider would have to draw upon the knowledge of one more learned than himself. Thus, under the cover of prevailing night, he retraced the route he had taken from the mountain retreat of Tex Barnes, savant.

* * * * *

Having recounted, over morning coffee and under a cerulean sky, all he had learned of Le Noir's devious commerce, the Ramrod Rider brought forth from his saddlebags the bottle of unknown liquid. At this discovery, the bard's eyebrows arched inquiringly. Upon administering a nasal probation, he drew those eyebrows close together.

"This is not common," he conceded. "I shall have to conduct research."

"I didn't aim to trouble you, Mister Barnes," urged the rider.

"It is no trouble, my young friend," returned the elder man. "My craft is one of enormous research, and I am interested in all things. Those cliff dwellings, for example, quite probably hold kernels of corn and shards of pottery, remnants of an ancient and noble culture. But those things later. Now it is the time to ask more urgent questions, as you have done. And it is to me, quite frequently, that people pose such questions. I have been fortunate to know more than the average man, and therefore I am expected to know the answers. I see myself as a funnel of knowledge through which vast information flows to those who seek it."

The scholar then betook himself into the recesses of the cave, emerging after some time with a volume that bore the signs of much perusing. "Father Pfefferkorn," he began, "lived and travelled throughout this region, and he has recorded many interesting findings in this volume. I have had recourse to it in the past. Hmmm . . . 'a large quantity of the poisonous juices from all kinds of the most malignant snakes, toads, scorpions, spiders, centipedes, and similar poisonous insects. To this are added . . .' —no," he interrupted himself, "this is on another matter." He made a small note to himself, presumably for future reference, and continued his search. At length he closed Father Pfefferkorn and returned to the bowels of the cave. Then he re-emerged with a volume entitled *A Complete Encyclopedia of Burial Procedures, Ancient and Modern.* After inexorable scrutiny, he laid his finger emphatically upon the right margin of the page to which the volume had been opened. "Here it is," he announced. "I think that what we have here is a sort of embalming fluid, designed to aid in the desiccation and mummification of the monkeys. I wouldn't be surprised," he said, with a reproachful glower in the general direction of the Frenchman's purlieu, "if those midgets are trained in administering this through syringes."

"What should we do?" posed the Ramrod Rider.

"We must avert wanton bloodshed at any cost," asserted the chronicler. "I have hated few men, but I am disgusted by the calloused motives of this Le Noir. We must foil his plans."

The rider cast a doubtful eye toward Tex Barnes. "You're not figurin' to get mixed up in this scrap, are you?"

"I have never been a day out of shape in my life," returned the writer, with some indignation, "but I can be of more assistance if I send word to some of my acquaintances, who live in the vicinity, and who share our desire to see law and order maintained. Go you, then, to those caves, and let yourself in secretly, and observe the intentions of those men. If worse comes to worst, and you must intervene to save the life of one of those unfortunate creatures, then so be it. Meanwhile, I will send help."

Thus it was that later that day, as the sun blazed in its brassy vault above, the Ramrod Rider found himself once again making a surveillance of the desert valley below him. By now the midgets had arrived on ponies, with a string of burros laden with panyards of supplies. These midgets, though fitted out in cowboy garb, comported themselves like interns or medics, which personnel the Ramrod Rider had observed in the Indian campaigns. They had the gait and carriage of careful, professional men, not the free and easy and sometimes bowlegged stride of cow-punchers. And so, if only for an instance, the Ramrod Rider appreciated Le Noir's mirth at the incongruity of these professionals masquerading as cowboys.

Just as the weary rider was beginning to tire of his toilsome post, he descried a bustle of activity. The midgets, assisted by Grubb and French Looie, were re-adjusting the packs on the burros. In a matter of fifteen minutes, the pack string was seen to embark in the direction of the caves, southward, led by Le Noir. Then the wagon train straightened out into a queue and accompanied the pack string, parallel to it, with the ungulate herd driven between the two columns and exhorted from behind by French Looie and Grubb. The midgets were driving the wagons; only Le Noir, ramrod straight in the saddle, was of the equestrian class.

This new development required swift thought on the part of the Ramrod Rider. He must trail safely at a distance, on the back side of a ridge, and then he must find a way into the caves where the iniquitous lucubrations were intended to transpire.

Having gained the crest of a slope looking down upon the newly formed camp of the conspirators, the rider quickly perceived that approach from the valley would be nigh impossible. He made a studied survey of the environs, and he concluded that his only way lay down the precipitous mountainside above the caves. If he were to let himself down a rope and onto a ledge of one of the upper caves, he might acquire a position of great advantage until Tex Barnes should send help. Seeing a sturdy juniper sprouting from the summit of the acclivity, he assured himself that there would be his route. Descending, he would swing into that one aperture, and there establish himself.

In the gathering of the evening, the Ramrod Rider tied his knot around the trunk of the juniper. It was his plan to descend at a point in time during which he could yet perceive the progress of his descent, but during which he would not be observed by the men below. Time was of the essence. At the precise moment he judged to be appropriate, he commenced; the first fifteen of the eighty feet were most difficult, as the rope lay fast against the granitic ledge. Thereafter, his progress was sure and steady, until he had arrived at a point about forty feet down the escarpment. He felt the rope twitch, and a small precipitation of dust and shale rattled upon his hat, attracting his attention upwards. His eyes quickly took in the sight of a glinting blade cutting, thread by thread, the hempen cord from which he hung pendant. The thin and curved poniard was grasped in a black-gloved hand. At the wrist, the sinister glove met a dusty, black silk cuff. Glinting also in the crepuscular light was a polished silver cuff link that bore the insignia of Le Noir Faineant.

The Ramrod Rider Looks into the Face of Destiny

If the Ramrod Rider were moderately perplexed by his earlier discoveries in this intrigue, he was, most certainly, exceedingly beleaguered at this moment. To hesitate would be to risk all. Risking rope-burn to hands that he would indubitably have use for in the near future, he slid down the rope, abating the friction with his feet pressed against the rope as brakes. Ten feet from the ledge he gave a slight swing inward, and he dropped safe onto the ledge. Still a hundred feet above the outlaw encampment, he wondered if Le Noir would follow him in person, or if that brigand would deploy his forces and direct them from a safe distance, paring his fingernails.

He was surprised: not by the descent of Le Noir, but by the cries of that execrable person. "Grubb!" he shouted. "Come up!"

The wary rider, craning his neck past the ledge and peering upward, made out in the evening light the forms of two men grappling on the verge of the mountaintop. One was clearly Le Noir Faineant, and the other, if the Ramrod Rider could accept the reality, was none other than Buffalo Waggens!

Some readers may recall William Wilberforce Waggens, y-clept Buffalo, that veteran plainsman and scout who had aided the Ramrod Rider in outwitting the notorious Durango Dan, a thrilling tale in itself that has been recorded elsewhere. To recapitulate briefly, however, this Buffalo Waggens was a shrewd but kindly man who had helped the Ramrod Rider in his hour of need, and here he was again, much to the surprise of the man who now stood on the ledge, looking upwards.

Even more to the surprise of the rider, there came bounding from the adjacent cave none other than Emmett Grubb, summoned by his patron. Seeing the Ramrod Rider, Grubb hesitated; then, with unexpected force, he flung the rider into the interior of the cave and began his upward climb. In a flicker, Buffalo Waggens slashed the rope with his Bowie, and Grubb was deposited on the ledge before he was three feet in the air. The rope itself slithered into a pile. Grubb turned his attention once again to the Ramrod Rider, who by this time was coming to his feet and acquainting himself with the formations of the cave. It was a small cave, about eight feet in depth and five feet in height, so that the rider came up in a crouch. As Grubb came rushing, the Ramrod Rider met him with a hearty blow to the neck. This staggered Grubb momentarily, but then he sprang, tiger-like, with renewed zeal to effect the defenestration of the Ramrod Rider. The latter, equally desperate to win, drove another fist at Grubb, this time to the throat, which dropped the outlaw flat. Quickly gathering up the cordage, the dexterous rider soon had his adversary trussed up like a calf for the branding.

The Ramrod Rider now re-directed his attention to the plight of Buffalo Waggens, who was audibly still struggling with the arch-villain Le Noir Faineant. As the rider came to the orifice of the cave to inquire upwards yet one more time, he heard the warning from above. "Look out below!" He drew himself back just in time, as he heard the rustling descent of an airborne body, clad in whispering silks, plunging to its reward.

In a matter of moments, Buffalo Waggens was on the ledge beside his younger friend, having in the meanwhile tied his own rope to the serviceable juniper and descended to join forces with his whilom trail pard.

"Well," said the Ramrod Rider. "I never expected to see you here. I thought we'd taken different trails after our last scrape."

"I just happened to be in this neck of the woods, young feller, and I sees this French guy, all dolled up in black, fixin' to cut a rope, and I wonders who or what might be on the other end of the rope, seein' as how it's stretched kinder tight, and blast my eyes if it ain't my young pard on the other end of that there rope."

The Ramrod Rider, gleaming with appreciation and warmth for his re-discovered friend, ejaculated, "I've never been happier to see someone in my whole life. I was in a fix when I saw you that time on the canyon rim when Durango Dan tried to cash in my chips, but now I'm even happier to see you as an old pard and as a friend in need."

"Yes," said the other, with a perceptible change in voice, and drawing off his hat and letting fall those venerable locks of hair recently impressed upon the perception of the Ramrod Rider, "I told you I was never a day out of shape in my life. Perhaps now I have made a believer out of you, my friend."

"Tex Barnes!" cried the rider, with the greatest incredulity he had known throughout this entire ordeal. "Tex Barnes! Is it really you? And what are you up to, pretendin' to be my old friend Buffalo Waggens? And how do you know about him?"

The savant raised his hand, Indian fashion. "We are one and the same. You have known me as two men: one as a man of thought and reflection, ostensibly sedentary and pensive; and one as a man of action, a man joined as one with nature, a man who has 'been to see the critter.' "

"Yes," ratified the rider. "Buffalo told me those very words the first time we met. And you are really both men? The two men I have admired most in my travels, and both the same? I don't understand."

"A man is like a diamond," began the sage. "He has many sides, many facets. Sometimes he shines from one, and sometimes he shines from another. And some day, perhaps at some future point along some future trail, we will meet again. For right now, I can say that while I have met you in two of my capacities, I have found you true and straight and always the same. You are a good man, a fighting man, a man who knows that cynicism is always the outward face of emptiness, a man who learns from the wisdom of others, a man who likes the feel of a good horse under him, the feel of a good rifle butt against his shoulder. And you have learned to be careful of building fires. When we meet again, perhaps I will instruct you in the care of walking on creeks that have been frozen over. But if that should occur, it will be at another time, another place. For now, it is good. There should be little said at time of parting."

With that pronouncement, Tex Barnes returned the hat to his head, smoothed out the cosmetically constructed features of Buffalo Waggens, and resumed the guise and demeanor of that worthy. Speaking again in the character of the amiable scout, and grasping the hand of the Ramrod Rider, he said, "Guess I'll shag on down the mountainside an' round up them other varmints. Got me a couple of young fellers down there handy with handcuffs. See you down there." He then hauled Emmett Grubb to his feet. "Come along, you owlhoot you," he prattled to the thug, who had just now made his return to consciousness, and who, thanks to the efforts of the Ramrod Rider, would now pay for the multitude of petty crimes that would be properly laid at his feet. With a lugubrious air, Grubb followed Buffalo Waggens along the ledge and out of sight.

The Ramrod Rider himself went back up the rope, the better to reconnoiter with his horse on the ridge-top. By the time the rider had gathered his mount and had made his way to the valley floor, Buffalo Waggens and his two assistants had already rounded up the wrong-doers, and they now had them mounted and handcuffed to their pommels, bound for incarceration. As Buffalo prepared to introduce the Ramrod Rider to these upholders of the law, the younger one, whose pistol handles bore inlaid figurines of blackbirds, pronounced, "My name's Carney Mc Crow, and they serve me aigs wherever I go." At this the rider marveled briefly, expecting further explication, but the young man was silenced by a chastening look from the paternal Buffalo.

The second man, whom Buffalo introduced as Gordon Pantry, expressed his pleasure at making the acquaintance of the Ramrod Rider; then, without further ceremony, he advised, "We'll send a detachment of troops to bring back the monkeys and goats. And was I you, I'd pull my freight—these are stolen Army wagons." Having rendered such laconic advice, he saluted.

In return, the central personage of our tale bestowed upon the group a tip of his Stetson and, receiving a knowing wink from Buffalo Waggens, resumed the trail down which further and unknown adventures no doubt lurked for the Ramrod Rider.

South of the Border
with the Ramrod Rider

NOTICE

Many anxious readers, having been enthralled by a volume entitled *Adventures of the Ramrod Rider*[*], have pressed solicitously for further details concerning the central figure of those narratives. Unfailingly observant that history repeats itself in the adventures of this stalwart rider of the mountains and plains, readers are eager to know about a link which seems to be missing in the earlier volume. That link is the Ramrod Rider of the second generation, whose career dates to the time of Herbert Hoover. The document that follows should prove a vital chapter in the chronicles of the man, bedecked in black, who called himself the Ramrod Rider.

[*]Which adventures have received widespread attention and acclaim and are, at the moment of this writing, being translated by divers hands into divers languages, notably *Las Aventuras del Ramrod Rider* and *Les Aventures du Ramrod Rider*, for the edification of readers around the world.

SOUTH OF THE BORDER
WITH THE RAMROD RIDER

Containing a Disquisition Upon Evil

Came a dark rider. Down from the wilds of New Mexico he rode, into the valley of the Río Grande where fruit trees and hayfields greened in the early summer sun. By midmorning the rider met with a dirt road, which he followed. This open road would be agreeable to the dark horse, which for two days had picked its way through yucca, prickly pear, creosote bush, and mesquite. The dirt road lay parallel to a paved road, which was a thoroughfare for the horseless carriages of the modern age—flivvers, roadsters, and trucks, which putted and roared and rattled by. Along the dirt road there was an equal share of traffic, less modern in aspect but all alive, slow-moving and liberally spaced. Over the space of four hours, the rider met with or passed up a variety of fellow creatures. He saw other riders, mounted on horse or burro, and he saw two-wheeled ox-carts, four-wheeled carriages, and freight wagons. Men walked leading pack animals—perhaps a burro with a large load of sticks, or a mule laden with sarapes. At times he passed a goatherd or a shepherd with a flock, and at other times he encountered simple pedestrians. All of these forms of life were moving from one spot on the warm earth to another, spots connected by a dusty strap of road that led to the west Texas town of El Paso. For it was this town, this international

46

city, that was the destination of the dark horseman, the man bedecked in black, who called himself the Ramrod Rider.

A dark rider, a lone rider, was this man in black, who rode the vast reaches of our great land in service of truth and justice. His was a life that did not know the pleasures of hearth and home, pretty wife, and lisping child; it was a life of dry camps, cold camps, small fires and no fires, dust on the backtrail and danger ahead. For the nonce, all he knew of the trail ahead was that in the teeming city of El Paso, or before that, or after that, there would present itself the need for justice to be served.

So it was that wherever he went, the Ramrod Rider kept a weather eye out for the odd and the covert. Injustice did not often display itself in the form of a town in flames, a gang of marauders, or the like. More often, as he had learned, it was the quiet work of a single man, in league with one or more lessers of his ilk. This man, under the cloak of respectability, moved in shadow. And to what purpose? The Ramrod Rider, if pressed, might have expounded two motives: gain for the self, and scorn for others. There seemed to be no end to such workers of evil. They sprouted up throughout the panoramic West, as if the grand artificer himself had sown the good earth with silver tokens stamped in his own image.

In his mission, therefore, the Ramrod Rider did not need an institution or an overseer. As a free agent of justice, he needed only to keep his eyes open, and sooner or later (usually not much later), the silver reptile raised its ugly head.

Into the town of El Paso he rode, crossing the broad highway and following a wide avenue, then turning onto an unpaved street, which dead-ended upon a narrower street, which in turn dead-ended upon a narrower and even more pocked and rutted street. The shadows of evening stretched onto the dusty passageway. Across the cool air came a song in Spanish, in a man's voice, which issued from a tavern called El Caballo Blanco. Down the street, still on the right side, was another tavern with an open door. Voices came from within, and a woman leaned in the doorway.

Down the street even farther, he found what he was look-ing for. It was a restaurant called El Nopal, much recommend-ed by cowpunchers, miners, freighters, and even sheepherders. It was a place of unassuming aspect, with a green cactus plant painted upon a smooth, whitewashed stucco wall, and the red letters of "El Nopal" bedaubed above the cactus.

Taking a seat by the window and mustering up his best cow-country Spanish, the Ramrod Rider soon had a beefsteak ranchero, a helping of mashed refried beans, and a small stack of steaming flour tortillas, the latter wrapped in a clean white towel. For his beverage the rider took ginger ale.

The restaurant El Nopal was a clean but not brilliantly lighted place. An ungenerous person might even have called it murky. Nonetheless, it gave one a chance to sit by a window and see outward without being sharply silhouetted.

Most of the passersby were dark-haired, dark-visaged, tranquil-looking folk dressed in bright colors. The rider saw two *señoritas* with long flowing hair, a young man with an armload of brooms, a mother leading a small boy, an older man pushing a fruit cart, two boys rolling a barrel hoop.

Then, at a moment when there was no traffic outside the window, the rider saw movement across the street. A door opened and a bell tingled, a man walked out, and the door closed. The man stood in front of the store and looked up and down the street, twice in each direction, as the light in the store behind him was extinguished. Then the man stepped into the street. He turned to his left and walked a few paces toward a brown horse that stood hipshot at a hitching rail. The man had something in his right hand. Peering intently, the Ramrod Rider determined that it was a bouquet of paint brushes of the tapering, thin-handled variety used by artists. The man patted the horse's neck with his left hand, then unbuckled the saddle bag and secured the paintbrushes. This much was not uncommon; but then, after once again looking sharply up and down the street, the man pulled his dusky brown hat down to his eyebrows, gathered his reins, swung into the saddle, and rode off into the gathering darkness.

Bright Lights and Poetry

The Ramrod Rider could not suppress his wonderment at what he had seen. As he had already reflected, the purchase of paintbrushes was not odd. Perhaps at this very moment, in the towns and cities across the nation and around the world, hundreds or even thousands of people were buying paintbrushes. But very few would be venturing furtively out into the street, with the air of having waited until sundown to make such an innocent purchase.

With his curiosity thus piqued, the Ramrod Rider mopped up his plate with the last tortilla, settled with the proprietor, and went out into the street. In the course of his rugged work, he had developed something akin to a sixth sense, an intuitive apprehension of things not being right. In obedience to that sense, he mounted his horse and continued in the direction he had been traveling earlier, which was also the direction taken by the suspicious stranger.

He could see the other man up the street two blocks. The man turned left onto a side street, as did the Ramrod Rider in his own good time. The man ahead turned right, as did the man who followed. Up ahead, the first man was tying his horse to a hitching rail on the left side of the street, where light streamed from the windows and the open door of a saloon. Drawing nearer, the Ramrod Rider observed a sign that identified the establishment as the Slender Sow. The lettering was quite elegant, as was the profile illustration of the sow herself, standing prim and upright on her hind trotters, with an open umbrella held by a front trotter and resting on her shoulder.

The sounds of laughter, piano music, spinning roulette wheels, and rattling poker chips carried out to the street. Bootheels thumped on the board sidewalk as men made their way inside. It seemed as if many men were arriving at the same time, as if for an event. Then the rider saw a poster next to the open door.

Declamation Tonight
8:00 P.M.
Cash Prizes

Intrigued, the rider dismounted, tied his horse, walked to the edge of the doorway, and peeked inward.

The furtive stranger was signing a register at a table, on the other side of which a pleasant young man with slicked-back hair sat attentively. The young man said, "You'll be contestant number five. And remember, even if you know your piece by heart, the presentation is to be done from a script."

The stranger nodded and took from an inside coat pocket a sheaf of papers.

The young man smiled. "You look like you're all set."

The stranger tucked the papers back into his coat and walked away without speaking.

The Ramrod Rider sank back from the light flooding outward through the doorway. He thought, whatever a declamation was, he should probably witness it. Furthermore, still guided by his sixth sense, he decided to make use of a disguise from his saddlebags.

In a matter of moments he was back at the doorway, a slouching man with a drooping mustache, fitted out in a battered hat, dusty miner's clothes, and lace-up boots.

"Name's Tombstone Tom," he said to the young man.

"Ready to declaim?"

"As ready as I'm likely to git." He bent as if to sign the register, and on the fifth line he saw a name written in a bold hand: *Daniel DuRonde*. He paused as if in thought.

"Something wrong, sir?"

"I just remembered something I forgot."

"Not your script, I hope."

"That's just it."

"Oh, my. I'm afraid you'd be disqualified."

"Of all the luck. What a thing to fergit. And me without my scripp."

"Well, sir, you're certainly welcome to sit in the audience and enjoy the competition."

"Think I might do just that." The Ramrod Rider then made his way further into the saloon, where he found a chair by itself and sat down. He raised his eyebrows and turned down the corners of his mouth, as if that were the proper demeanor when waiting for a declamation to begin.

Presently the show was under way, with a few pleasant words from the young man by way of introducing the event and the first speaker. Soon enough, the Ramrod Rider understood that a declamation was a loud delivery of poetry, a thundering of rhyme accompanied by blazing eyes and a shaking fist. The contestant wept about a girl named Lenore and wailed about a crow that wouldn't go away.

This fellow can't win, thought the rider; *he repeats himself too much.*

The next contestant thundered likewise about a brigade of soldiers that rode into the jaws of death. He repeated himself less, but he crumpled his papers badly and left the air in front of him scarred with his long index fingernail.

Contestant number three, after some apology, also wept about Lenore. His sorrow seemed to be divided—half of it proceeding from lost Lenore, and half of it from the circumstance of not being the first to mourn her this evening.

The fourth contestant improved the Ramrod Rider's notion of what a declamation might consist of. This contestant bit his lip, shook his head, seethed his *s*'s, and did a fair imitation of the sound of horse hooves on hard ground. His story, delivered in a suspenseful voice, was about a highwayman and his dark-eyed sweetheart. This was a dashing story, with love and daring and treachery, all measured out in poetry that trotted and galloped. The Ramrod Rider felt himself lifted—nay, transported—by the delivery, until at the end of the declamation he returned to an awareness of himself. Only then did he know again that he was in the international city of El Paso, that he was in the guise of Tombstone Tom, and that he was one of an audience that had been caught up by the magic of poetry.

The fifth and last contestant, Daniel DuRonde, was next introduced. The Ramrod Rider, consciously in the manner of Tombstone Tom, observed the speaker. Beneath the drab brown hat, now pushed back, sparkled a pair of sharp blue eyes. The clean-shaven face was fair-skinned and rosy, with wide, prominent cheekbones. The man's hair was a dull blond, shot with silver. A cookie-duster mustache danced on his upper lip as he spoke.

"Although I run the risk of seeming immodest, tonight I presume to deliver a work of my own composing. With all respect to the work of the masters, I present: 'When My Pony Sheds Again.' "

The Ramrod Rider marveled at even this much, for the speaker ended his introduction with a flourish that seemed to lift the whole room. Then with an electric voice, the man in command of the audience began the declamation.

When My Pony Sheds Again

I've been west to California,
    I've been north to Idaho
I've been east to old Virginia,
    I've been south to Mexico.

But of all the spots I've been to
    There's a place I love the best,
In the heart of the Rocky Mountains,
    In the distant cold northwest.

'Neath the sky of old Montana,
    On the banks of Powder Creek,
Lives a brave and honest trapper
    With his daughter Angelique.

She has cheeks as white as ivory,
    Framed in silky long black hair,
And her eyes are blue as lupine

ADVENTURES OF THE RAMROD RIDER

That adorns the meadows there.

Across the valley is my cabin,
    Just a humble twelve-by-ten,
Where I hope to hang my saddle
    When my pony sheds again.

It was on a bright May morning
    That I kissed her on the cheek
And with many a tear and promise
    Took my leave of Angelique.

Safe inside an empty watch-case
    In the pocket of my vest
Was a lock of hair she gave me,
    In response to my request—

For not once in eighteen summers
    On the banks of Powder Creek
Had a person with a camera
    Photographed my Angelique.

Nor had any other artist
    Ever drawn or painted her—
Never brushed her hair on canvas,
    Never sketched her smile demure.

Thus inside my golden watch case
    Tied in thread and wrapped with care

Was my version of a portrait
     In a lock of raven hair.

And I told her as I kissed her
     That when once my furs were sold,
I would pledge her my devotion
     With a diamond set in gold.

Then we said good-bye that morning
     And I left her all alone,
As I led the pack mules eastward
     To the banks of the Yellowstone,

Where I trailed along the river
     'Midst the herds of buffalo
And cut east towards Dakota
     Through the land of the Sioux and Crow.

At the campfire every evening
     'Neath the silver stars of night
I recalled my blue-eyed darling
     With her blushing cheeks of white.

And as if to see her picture,
     With a motion soft as prayer,
I would open up the watch-case
     To behold her beauty there.

Then beneath the starry heavens

ADVENTURES OF THE RAMROD RIDER

I would lay me down to rest,
There to dream of one girl only
    Who was waiting in the west.

Each new dawn would find me stirring,
    Loading up the mules again,
To resume my travel eastward
    On across the endless plain.

Then I crossed the famous Badlands,
    Where the coyotes wailed at night,
And the buzzards wheeled in circles
    In the sky so vast and bright.

Oh, it made a man feel little
    In a land so vast and spare,
And I prayed to God in heaven
    Not to let me perish there—

But to help me cross the Badlands
    And escape the vulture's beak,
So that I might sell my plunder
    And return to Powder Creek.

But before I left the Badlands,
    On a warm and breathless day,
I observed another horseman
    Who was headed north my way.

He came riding from the Badlands
    On a horse as black as coal,
Like a skiff upon the ocean
    As the waves beneath it roll—

For the billows of the prairie
    Seemed to move beneath the shape
Of the loping mounted horseman
    In his flowing dusky cape.

He had silver spurs that jingled
    And a flat-crowned charcoal hat;
The pearl handle on his six-gun
    Matched the pin on his cravat.

He had one continuous eyebrow
    And a pair of gimlet eyes,
But a smile so warm and friendly
    That it took me by surprise.

My new friend fell in beside me
    With the jingle of his spurs
As I led my pack mules onward
    With my winter's catch of furs.

For three nights we camped together,
    Shared a fire upon the trail,
Rolled our blankets out like brothers,
    With no hint of his betrayal.

Then upon the third bleak morning
 As I rose to greet the day,
He was gone like cold grey ashes
 That the wind has swept away.

He was gone with horse and bedroll,
 By the dawn's first rosy streak,
And my blood ran cold as water
 As I thought of Angelique—

For the night before, at moonrise
 As I settled down to rest,
I had folded up my clothing
 And on top had put my vest.

Now the early daylight showed me
 Where this thief had made his play—
He had pillaged my gold watch-case
 From my waistcoat where it lay.

No doubt thinking it had value,
 For it looked like an antique,
He had robbed me of my treasure—
 He had stolen Angelique.

Now the smold'ring hate within me
 Leapt ablaze like burning pitch,
And the only thought I nurtured

Was to kill that sonofab----.

But before I could get vengeance
 I would have to sell my furs,
To have money and provisions
 As I tracked those silver spurs.

I made haste from that day onward,
 By the light of sun and moon,
Till I reached the broad Missouri
 On the fifteenth day of June.

First I sold my pile of beaver
 Then the mules and all the gear,
Filled my warbag with provisions
 And then headed north to Pierre.

All along the trail I questioned
 Every man I chanced upon,
And the answers pointed northward
 As I learned where he had gone.

Through that rough Dakota country
 Night and day I traced his route,
Till I lost his trail completely
 At a place called Thunder Butte.

On a hunch I headed southward,
 Always looking for my man,

ADVENTURES OF THE RAMROD RIDER

Till another fortnight brought me
    To the cowtown called Cheyenne.

There as always I asked questions,
    And at length to my surprise
I was told about a stranger
    With a pair of gimlet eyes.

Yes, his silver spurs did jingle,
    And he wore a charcoal hat,
And the handle of his six-gun
    Matched the pearl on his cravat.

In Cheyenne he was remembered
    Though he stayed for just one day,
And he said he soon expected
    To go back to Santa Fe.

Down through Denver, then, I tracked him,
    Always dreaming of the day
I would come upon this scoundrel
    And at last would make him pay.

But my dreams remained elusive,
    For pursue him as I might,
He was like a fleeting shadow,
    Out of reach and out of sight.

So the summer slipped to autumn

As I clung to my belief
That the trail ahead would shorten
As I stalked this phantom thief.

But the tracks were always faded,
And the campfire coals were dead,
And no matter how I hurried,
He remained one camp ahead.

Now his trail leads through the mountains
To the west of Santa Fe,
And the sun is slipping southward
With the dying of each day.

And my horse's coat grows thicker
As the days grow short and cold,
And my rifle seems so heavy
And the reins so hard to hold.

As the soft white snow comes falling
I can feel it on my cheek,
And it takes me back in memory
To the banks of Powder Creek.

But the sullen hope within me
Drives me daily on my way
To seek justice for a girl who
Lives a thousand miles away.

If it takes me through the winter,
    I will track him down and then
Be back home in old Montana
    When my pony sheds again.

Small Potatoes

A thundering response shook the chandeliers of the Slender Sow, as the members of the audience applauded, cheered, and beat their bootheels upon the wooden floor. The man of the hour, Daniel DuRonde, folded his manuscript, tucked it back into his jacket, and tipped his hat. His eyes swept the crowd and, as it seemed, rested for a second on Tombstone Tom, who squirmed his mustaches and took a deep breath. Then as the applause ended, the final contestant took a seat in an empty chair in front of Tom.

Before long, the young man who served as impresario appeared before the crowd and announced the judges' decision. The winner was contestant number five, Daniel DuRonde, who stood and tipped his hat to a second round of applause, less forceful than the first but appreciable all the same. The young man informed the winner that the prize money would be available in a few minutes; DuRonde nodded and moved to the bar.

The Ramrod Rider, still consciously in the guise of Tombstone Tom, watched as the man in the brown hat signaled for a bottle and then, with his right side away from the bar, poured a drink with a steady left hand. He lifted the small glass to eye level, holding it aloft with his thumb and first two fingers, then downed his drink in one smooth motion and twirled the glass as he set it on the bar. Glancing at the table near the entrance, where the young man once again sat, DuRonde gave a sign of recognition, nodded, and moved away from the bar.

Fortuitously, the table was within earshot of Tombstone Tom, who sat staring at his miner's boots. He glanced up and saw the young man handing an envelope to the winning contestant.

"Here it is, sir," said the young man. "The grand prize."

The recipient had his back to Tombstone Tom, but the words were audible. "Small potatoes," he said. "But, as they say, *il faut manger*." With no further grace, the winner walked out the door, leaving the young man with mouth agape and a puzzled look on his face.

Tombstone Tom rose and stretched, yawning and then rubbing his eyes. Then he scratched the back of his neck, blinked, hitched his trousers, and trudged out of the well-lit saloon into the dark night. Once out of the light cast through the open doorway, he moved quickly to his horse, finding everything as he had left it. As he watched the departing figure of Daniel DuRonde, he lost no time in shucking his disguise and becoming once again the Ramrod Rider in full detail. Then he was aboard the dark horse and trailing the mysterious stranger, who seemed to be heading toward the border.

No guards emerged from the check station on the other side of the bridge until DuRonde stopped his horse and called out two syllables. Then a man of military aspect emerged from the station, which was on the right-hand side of the bridge. He

approached the rider, who leaned, shook his hand, straightened up, saluted, and rode on.

The Ramrod Rider, who had paused, let the rider move
ahead before he himself continued across the bridge. As he
approached the small building, he saw four men sitting in a
cloud of tobacco smoke, playing cards beneath an overhead
kerosene lamp.

"*Bueno*," he called out.

No one stirred.

"*Bueno*," he called again.

At length one of the men played a card, then laid his hand
of cards face down on the table, stood up, slung a rifle on his
shoulder, and walked outside.

The Ramrod Rider leaned over, shook the proffered hand,
and seated himself properly again in the saddle. As he raised
his hand in salute, he noticed that the guard was looking down
at his own empty palm. Then he looked up at the rider, made
half a motion in the direction of a salute, and waved him
onward. And so the Ramrod Rider crossed the border into
Mexico.

The rider ahead did not go through the center of town but
rather skirted it two blocks to the left. After perhaps a dozen
blocks southward, he turned again to the right, never looking
back, and rode several blocks westward, past a plaza and a
very large church with two towers, and then turned left. He
rode southward for quite a ways as the land rose upward.
Human habitations began to thin out, and at the edge of the
populated neighborhood, tucked against a rising hillside, was
situated a large house.

Because of the distance and the darkness, the Ramrod Rider could not be sure, but the house seemed to be a stuccoed, one-story building. Lights were burning behind several windows, so even at a distance the perceptive rider could discern an iron railing that stood between the house and the world at large.

The lead rider approached this railing and apparently tapped on it with a metallic object, for the summons was clearly audible at a hundred yards' distance. Within a minute could be heard a rattling at the gate, then the squeaking sound of a gate being opened, a few short syllables, the clop of hooves on a paved courtyard, and the squeaking clang of the gate closing.

Now did the Ramrod Rider ponder. He wondered if he should continue following the dictates of his own heart, which told him that the secretive Daniel DuRonde was up to some business that did not serve the best interests of humankind. Then his thought took the other direction, as he questioned his right to pursue and observe. He called for the evidence that justified his actions, and in review, there were but two details—nay, three. First, there was the furtive acquisition of paintbrushes; second, the supercilious manner in which the man accepted the prize for his declamation; and third, the curious circumstance of his having taken an inconspicuous route to his stronghold across the border.

The Ramrod Rider nodded to himself as he stood by his horse in the darkness. He would follow his heart, which told him there was no such thing as small potatoes in the service of truth and justice.

King Tut Tries to Queer the Deal

Having thus satisfied himself, the Ramrod Rider retraced his route until he came to a small café he had noticed. Light emanated from an open door, so that the rider could see, painted upon a tan stuccoed wall, the words "La Rosa Blanca," and beneath that, a single white rose upon a graceful upright stem.

Entering La Rosa Blanca, the rider was greeted by a kindly couple, old enough to be his parents but not yet aged and infirm. They showed him to a table, and through the *lingua franca* of their limited English and his limited Spanish, he gave them to understand that he did not care to eat at the present but would enjoy a soda.

The refreshment being served, the three engaged further in halting conversation, until the Ramrod Rider let it be known that he had crossed the border with the purpose of knowing more about a man who lived in the neighborhood.

—Oh, yes, they said. The gringo on the hill.

It had occurred to the curious rider that the aforesaid gringo might keep to this side of the border because of domestic interests. Again in the *patois* of cow-country Spanish, he asked if the man had a wife and family.

—Oh, no. He lives alone.

—Alone alone? The rider remembered there being a gatekeeper of sorts.

—He has working for him one man. *El dolicocéfalo.*

—Who?

—*El dolicocéfalo.*

The rider shook his head.

The host then gave a brief explanation in fluent Spanish, of which the rider captured only one word.

—*¿Cabeza?* he queried.

Now the hostess joined in, and with one hand above her dark wavy hair and the other beneath her chin, she conveyed the idea of a long head. Then pressing with both hands against her cheekbones, she gave the idea of a narrow head.

—Like the horse, said the host, pointing at the seated guest.

—Me?

—No. The other man. He has a head like your horse.

—Oh. The Ramrod Rider pictured a servant with the body of a man and the head of a horse. He nodded.

The host and hostess then transmitted the intelligence that in the morning would come to this place a young man who did work for the gringo on the hill.

The Ramrod Rider expressed his interest in meeting the young man. Then, upon inquiring for a place to lodge himself and his exemplary horse, meanwhile paying for his soda, he was led around back to a stable. There, in the pleasant company of burros and goats and chickens, did rest come to the dark horse and dark rider.

* * * * *

In the morning, at the breakfast table in La Rosa Blanca, The Ramrod Rider made the acquaintance of the young man,

Ramiro. He spoke perfect English, and he explained that the kindly couple were his aunt and uncle—Tía María and Tío Tomás. He went on to explain that he was contracted to install window grates on Daniel DuRonde's house.

The usually cautious rider felt that here was a man to be trusted. Ramiro, in addition to being of about the same age, height, and weight as the Ramrod Rider, also radiated an aura of frankness and sincerity. Thus, when Ramiro said he understood that the visitor had some interest in the house on the hill, the Ramrod Rider acknowledged his suspicions.

"Come with me, then," said Ramiro. "You can pose as my assistant."

"In these clothes?" countered the rider.

"I have others," laughed Ramiro. "And you have a good enough sun tan that no one will know the difference."

This much was true, for, sooth to say, the Ramrod Rider was richly tanned from his life in the great outdoors.

"Very well," said the rider. "Now, tell me. Who is the long-headed servant who works for DuRonde?"

Ramiro laughed. "You must mean Whit. You'll get a look at him."

"Whit?"

"His name is Whit Whitmore. As you might expect from the name, he is North American. But he was abandoned and grew up here, in the streets of Juárez, so he speaks very bad English." Ramiro sipped his coffee and cocked his head. "Actually, he speaks pretty bad Spanish, too."

"Uh-huh," said the the rider. "And what kind of work will you have me doin'?"

"I have a can of black paint and some paint brushes, and you can paint the iron work on the windows."

"Doesn't the owner furnish the brushes?"

"Oh, no," answered Ramiro, assuming an air of dignity. "As an independent contractor, I provide my own brushes."

* * * * *

The morning sun was warm as the contractor and his assistant, the latter garbed in the cotton drab and straw sombrero of the laborer, trudged along the dusty road. As they climbed the hill leading to the DuRonde hacienda, the Ramrod Rider observed a human figure in the courtyard behind the six-foot railing.

"Is that the long-headed fellow?"

"Yes, that is Whit Whitmore."

Drawing closer, the Ramrod Rider determined that Whitmore was sweeping the courtyard. Yet closer, he observed the man's head.

It was not grotesquely long, as a horse's head would be upon a human body, but it was a noticeably long head, crowned with a dirty mop of blond hair. He looked like an animal in a cage, until he leaned his broom against the railing and opened the gate. Now the Ramrod Rider observed a pair of pale blue eyes widening downward, a flat nose, and a lantern jaw.

"*Buenoh díah, maestro,*" said the lackey.

"*Buenos días,*" answered Ramiro, who nodded and walked through the gateway.

The Ramrod Rider was about to utter a similar greeting when he saw the horse head turn away, as if it were beneath the dignity of a gatekeeper to speak to an iron worker's apprentice. Thus relieved, the Ramrod Rider lowered his hatbrim and walked through.

Before long, the apprentice was standing on a wooden crate and thoughtfully applying black paint to a window grate. Much to his satisfaction, the window was opened inward, presumably for ventilation.

Across the room, seated in a chair beside a table that held a kerosene lamp, was the man from the night before. Now hatless, and dressed in a black silk robe or housecoat, he was sipping coffee and reading a book. The apprentice made out the title of the book to be *The Time Machine*, and the book seemed to hold the reader's attention. At one point, without altering the position of the book, the lord of the manor called for his servant and ordered more coffee.

It occurred to the Ramrod Rider that the master was so accustomed to servants that he could ignore any of them, including an iron worker's apprentice.

Whitmore came and went on various errands, and presently the Ramrod Rider became aware that there was a room in back of the one he looked into. The hammer-headed attendant slipped into and out of this room without opening the door wide, as if he were more aware of an onlooker than the master was.

The Ramrod Rider stepped down from his perch. A little less than an hour had elapsed, and he had two of the five bars painted. Laying his brush across the top of the paint can, he hitched his cotton trousers and walked around the house, as if to answer the exigencies of nature.

There, as he expected, he saw an adobe extension of the house, less pleasing cosmetically than the façade that looked upon the world. Furthermore, the back side of the house was built right up to the hillside, which rose at this point as a rock escarpment.

The adobe wall had one small window, with rusted bars fixed in the window frame itself. A dull light glowed within.

Stepping quietly, the Ramrod Rider approached the window, and keeping to one side, peered through the dirty pane of glass.

It was a large room, extending to the observer's left and back into a cave, the recesses of which were indistinguishable. In the forefront of the room, almost directly in front of the window, was a long work table with two lanterns hanging overhead. Seated at the table, much to the rider's surprise, he saw a dozen Chinese. In the camps and bunkhouses of his travels, the stalwart rider had seen here and there a Chinese cook or launderer, so he recognized immediately the small cap, the braided hair, and the gown. But here were a dozen, and working at an unusual occupation; for each had before him a plaster of Paris figure of a seated Mexican sleeping with his hatted head upon his knees. The Chinese workmen were painting the figures, giving them all blue trousers, red shirts, and yellow sombreros. The Ramrod Rider pursed his lips as he surveyed the scene, and then his eyes rested on a cylindrical crock at the end of the table. It held half a dozen fresh, unused paintbrushes.

He felt his mouth open in wonderment. Then he closed his mouth, swallowed, nodded to himself, and returned to his work.

As he was painting the third bar on the window, he saw the master lay down the book he had been reading. After a meditative pause, the man got up, crossed the room out of the apprentice's view, and returned to his easy chair with another book.

Opening the book, he intoned, "*Je suis.*"

The apprentice lowered his head and listened. This must be French, he thought, like the phrase from the night before.

The sonorous voice continued. "*Je suis. Je suis le patron.*" A pause was followed by, "*Vous êtes. Vous êtes une femme.*" Then came a clearing of the throat, and, "*Il est. Il est malade. Il est toujours malade.*" Then there was another pause, and the pronouncement, "*Je suis. Je suis à côté de la fenêtre.*"

The Ramrod Rider peeked through the window, and he saw the man still seated, with an intense look on his face. Wishing to remain inconspicuous, the apprentice moved his wooden stand and resumed painting the last bar as he stood to the side of the window.

Next he was aware of Whit Whitmore behind him in the courtyard, in answer to a tapping at the railing. There was an exchange in English, and in another moment Whitmore appeared before his master, as the apprentice's eyesight cleared the windowsill.

"He is here, the man with the truck."

"You mean King Tut?"

"Dyess."

"Well, show him in, then." As Whitmore turned and left the room, DuRonde closed his French book and muttered, still in his French voice, "*Cochon.*" Then he rose from his chair, smoothed his robe, and wrinkled his nose.

The apprentice went on painting.

Before long, a stranger entered the room. He was of average height or a little above, heavy-set, and clean. He had brown wavy hair, neatly cut, and he was clean-shaven. He had clear blue eyes, and a glint of cruelty shone in his face as he smiled. Having seen this much, the Ramrod Rider withdrew and listened as he continued to paint.

"Mr. DuRonde," said the visitor.

"Mr. Tutweiler. We meet again. Please sit down."

"Thank you."

"Cigar?"

"No, thank you."

"Brandy?"

"No, thank you."

"Coffee?"

"Why, that sounds fine. That doesn't interfere with the Lord's work."

"Whit, bring us some coffee."

"*Sí, señor*—uh, dyessir."

"Well, Mr. Tutweiler, do make yourself comfortable."

"Thank you."

"Pleasant trip?"

"More or less. I left my truck at the bottom of the hill. I didn't want it to heat up any more than it had to."

"A wise decision, no doubt."

"I thought so." At this point King Tut cleared his throat and said, "I hope them Chinamen got here all right."

"The Celestials? Yes, they did. And I have them happily ensconced."

"I suppose they can walk down the hill, then."

"Not right away."

"Oh?"

"I have some work for them to do."

"What do you mean?"

"I've arranged for them to do some painting."

"Looked like a regular greaser to me."

"What? Oh, no. Those are just day laborers. The Celestials are back in here. Let me show you."

The Ramrod Rider heard the two men get up and cross the room. The door opened, and a minute later it closed. Then he heard the two men return to their seats.

"I don't get it," said King Tut. "What's the purpose?"

"Just a little profit on the side. Once they get this far—across the ocean in a ship, across the mountains on the train, and then up the desert on another train—they can't quite refuse to put in a few days' work here at my resort."

"You mean you're just squeezin' some free labor out of 'em."

"You put it so bluntly."

"What're you gonna do with that painted junk, then?"

"Each Celestial can carry two of them across the river, so I get a little tax-free importing done while I'm at it." After a pause, DuRonde laughed and added, "Call it my version of the white man's burden."

"Uh?"

"Never mind."

"Well, I don't like it."

"What's it to you?"

"I contracted to haul a load of these pigtails to the border. I didn't agree to haul a bunch of tourist junk for free along with 'em, and I don't want to wait for my cut."

"Don't get your hackles up."

"I came to haul these Chinamen today, and I want to get paid today to do it, and that's that."

"Now see here, Mr. Tutweiler. Don't think we're going to do things your way just because you want to. I can get anyone to deliver these Celestials to the border, but you can't get paid, and neither can that horse thief Brogan, on the other side, except through me."

"I don't like to be talked to like that."

"You don't have to like it. I brought you in as a subordinate, not as some upstart who thinks he's going to be the boss—no, not one whit!"

"Dyess?"

"Not you, you idiot. I thought you were supposed to be making coffee."

"Dyessir."

"Well, then," said King Tut, "I just might take my truck to Colorado and make a quick thousand or so haulin' sugar beets."

"That might be the best place for you."

"It just might be."

The Ramrod Rider heard the squeak of one chair and the scrape of another, accompanied by DuRonde's peremptory "Whit!"

"Dyess?"

"Show Mr. Tutweiler to the door. Forget about the coffee."

"Dyessir."

The apprentice was now painting the underside of the bars where they stuck out from the house before turning upward. He heard the iron gate clang behind him, and a moment later he heard Whitmore's voice from within the room.

"The man, he is berry mat."

"I suppose he is."

"You don' wanna work fer da King?"

"I don't work for any king, you idiot, or for anyone else, for that matter." The apprentice straightened up and caught a glimpse of the man in the silk robe thumbing his own sternum. "I ride for the Double Dee."

"Dyessir."

"Remember that."

"Dyess."

The Ramrod Rider lowered himself again, and after some pause he heard the servant's voice. As always, he found it incongruous to hear such fractured English coming from a person who, by his looks, should speak at least as well as a person from Missouri. The man said, "Who you gonna git now for to carry these Chinies?"

77

"I don't know. Anyone with a truck. It seems like the country's full of burros, but I've seen a few trucks. Do you know of anyone, offhand, who has a truck?"

"Dyust the gringo Dyeemee."

Capture—and Escape

By mid-day the Ramrod Rider had painted two complete window grates from top to bottom and all around. As he and Ramiro trudged down the hill toward La Rosa Blanca, he told the artisan of what he had learned.

"Oh, yes," said Ramiro. "Your country now has a quota on how many Chinese may come in through the ports. There is still no control in Mexico, so they come in great numbers and then sneak into the U.S. There are some people who fly them in airplanes, also."

"Airplanes!"

"Yes, indeed. You've seen an airplane, haven't you?"

"Well, yes, once."

"This man DuRonde would be even harder to catch then."

"We've got enough to do to try to stop him now," said the rider.

"Yes, we do."

During the mid-day meal, the Ramrod Rider and his ally devised a plan. Ramiro would alert the border authorities on the American side (for there was nothing illegal transpiring in terms of Mexican law), and he would be prepared to ride to notify them on the day of the attempted delivery. His apprentice, meanwhile, would attempt a career change and seek work with the gringo Yeemee.

Tía María and Tío Tomás offered to provide an introduction for the Ramrod Rider. Every afternoon, as Ramiro explained it, they sent a helper to purchase flour and lard, and this worthy would show the way to Yeemee's residence.

The plan thus agreed upon, Ramiro returned to his work at the DuRonde stronghold, while the Ramrod Rider, in his original clothes once again, awaited the arrival of the man who fetched provisions.

This man, he learned from Tía María, was named Tlacuache.

"Meanin'?" queried the rider.

"Ees animal," replied Tía María. She snapped her head to one side and closed her eyes, saying, "Esleep too much."

The Ramrod Rider imagined, then, a person with a long snout, ugly hands and feet, and some version of a bare tail. What he met instead was a person who corresponded in physiognomy to the other features of the animal so aptly characterized by Tía María.

Tlacuache was a rotund, cheerful fellow of about thirty, with bristly hair and a bristly mustache. Talkative, he gave a diluted, circumstantial explanation which the Ramrod Rider in turn distilled into the notion that Tlacuache went here and there and everywhere with his *diablito*, or hand truck, and carried things for people. Every afternoon he passed by here, received an order from the proprietors of La Rosa Blanca, and then fetched a day's supply of flour and lard, which was apparently enough to merit a *diablito*.

The hand truck was presently loaded with firewood, which, Tlacuache explained, he would deliver to a señora who lived near Yeemee, who used it to boil corn in a large square can, for the purpose of making corn tortillas. La Rosa Blanca, of course, specialized in flour tortillas, and for that reason he went every day for flour and lard.

The Ramrod Rider nodded throughout this exchange of intelligence, and when Tlacuache rose from the table, the rider did also, following the cheerful guide out into the street where the *diablito* stood waiting.

On through the streets they rumbled, in the opposite direction from la casa DuRonde. Tlacuache steered with one hand and helped himself speak with the other. He told about the people from the south, the *yucatecos*, who were short and had large heads. *Cabezón*, he said. Large head. He stopped the *diablito* so that he might speak with both hands, holding them out beside his ears, as if balancing a globe on his shoulders. As they resumed their trek, Tlacuache, who was not very tall himself, held his arm straight out to signify the shortness of the southern cousins. The Ramrod Rider nodded, imagining distant relatives a meter in height, with heads the size of prize-winning pumpkins.

Tlacuache talked on, venturing to say that the gringo Yeemee was very fat, and much tolerated by his wife and her family. Yeemee was always drunk, he said, but the truck was a good business. And furthermore, everyone loved Yeemee very much.

Finally pointing out the place, Tlacuache rumbled onward with his load of firewood, while the Ramrod Rider found himself facing a nondescript adobe dwelling. There were no windows on the front of the hut, and the wooden doorway seemed to have lost its door, as there was a blanket tacked to the lintel or cross beam of the door frame.

The Ramrod Rider knocked on the rough wooden door jamb. He knocked again. Then he picked up a stone at his feet and used it to knock more loudly. He stood back as a brown hand moved the blanket aside.

The owner of the hand was a plump, dark woman with a full head of hair and a small nose.

"Jess?"

"No, that ain't me," said the rider, "nor the man I'm lookin' for. I'm lookin' for Jimmy."

"*¿Yimi?*"

"Yes. *Sí.*"

The *señora* regarded him narrowly and then shook her head.

"Yeemee," said the rider, showing with his hands that he meant a large person. Then he showed the palms of his hands, signifying a person of light complexion. "Yeemee," he repeated.

"*Un momento,*" said the *señora*, who ducked back into the dwelling. In a moment she re-emerged with a ten-year-old boy, pudgy and squinting, whom she thrust in front of her.

The boy spoke. "She say Yeemee is berry tire and will see him better to you tomorrow."

From the background there came pidgin execrations, a voice muttering in a mixture of English and Spanish, which, as nearly as the Ramrod Rider could decipher, referred to sons of a bedbug pinching flies.

"Yeemee?" queried the rider, motioning in the direction of the sound.

The boy looked up at the woman, who put her hands together beneath her ear and tilted her head. "*Dormido*," she said.

"Asleep," said the rider.

"Jess," said the boy. "He esleep. Better you come tomorrow."

* * * * *

On the morrow morn, the Ramrod Rider appeared again at the adobe hut and tapped on the door jamb with a stone. The same woman appeared, then disappeared wordlessly, and in her place the doorway was filled with a person who could be none other than Yeemee. He had cropped brown hair, bloodshot eyes, and yellow teeth—all in contrast with his pallid, doughy face. He wore a short-sleeved undershirt and a pair of bib overalls, which were stretched to a full sesquimeter of girth.

"They told me some white man was lookin' fer me," he said. "I suppose you're the same one."

"That I am," said the rider. "Name's Tom."

The other man made no move to shake hands but merely asked, as he grimaced, "What kin I do fer ya?"

"I'm lookin' fer work. I'm a swamper."

The large man gave him what might have been a dubious look. "What can you do?"

"Anything a swamper needs to do—buck bales, stack bags, carry shingles up a ladder, dump coal in a basement, prod cattle, and gopher."

"Gopher what?"

"Go fer whatever the boss sends me for."

"You sound like a real swamper to me. I might could use you. It so happens I got some freight to haul tomorrow."

* * * * *

And so the stage was set. The following morning, the Ramrod Rider returned as scheduled. With a broom borrowed from the *señora*, he swept out the canopied back of the truck; with a long screwdriver, he dislodged ancient gobs of mud from the underside of the vehicle; and with a leaky galvanized bucket, he washed the whole exterior.

Not until after the mid-day mealtime and siesta hour did Yeemee emerge from the house. Perhaps surmising correctly that the swamper knew nothing about machines, or perhaps not wanting to yield any authority to a swamper, he turned on the ignition, set the hand throttle, shook the gearshift to make sure it was in neutral, pulled the hand brake one click tighter, took the crank from behind the seat, and walked to the front of the truck. There he inserted the crank and positioned himself, hovering a second and then sagging down on the crank.

The engine creaked and popped.

The operator re-positioned the crank and leaned onto it again. This time the engine popped, grunted, and sputtered into life. Yeemee extracted the crank and lumbered back to the cab, where he flung the crank behind the seat.

"Git in," he hollered above the noise of the engine.

The swamper climbed in and sat on a doubled burlap bag, which provided some protection against the bare springs.

"Gotta adjust the choke," said the driver.

"Uh-huh."

"Delicate things, these machines."

"Uh-huh."

"But you treat 'em right, an' they do all the work."

"Uh-huh."

"My thinkin' is, don't ever haul nothin' that don't run in and out by itself."

"Uh-huh."

"That's cattle and sheep—or gasoline, if you got one of them trucks."

"Uh-huh."

"Today we're haulin' live freight."

"Uh-huh."

"When we git to where we're gonna load up, you stay in the cab and keep yer mouth shut. When we git to where we're goin', you kin help unload."

"Uh-huh."

"And then you kin sit in the truck and keep an eye on it, 'cause I got a couple places I wanna stop on the way back. You got that, swamper?"

"Uh-huh."

Yeemee put the truck into motion and drove without incident until he came to the bottom of the hill below DuRonde's house. The truck gave a couple of violent lurches until the driver put it into the correct gear for climbing the grade. The truck groaned up the hill, and with some maneuvering at the top, the driver got the vehicle turned around and backed up to the house. Then he set the hand brake.

"You see this pedal right here?" he said. "It's the foot brake. If this thing starts to roll, you step on it."

"Uh-huh."

"Now you wait here."

In a few minutes the swamper heard commotion and felt movement as the live freight boarded the truck. Then he heard Yeemee's voice.

"How long ago did he leave?"

Whitmore's voice answered. "Barely almost more than an hour."

"On a horse?"

"Dyess."

"Well, I reckon we'll git there at the same time."

The driver climbed into the cab, released the brake, put the vehicle in gear, and ground forward. As they hit the downhill grade, he put the truck out of gear and let it coast, which it did admirably until it hit a chuck hole at the bottom. The swamper hit his head on the ceiling, and as he did so, he heard thumping in the back which suggested that more than one piece of plaster of Paris would need to be swept out later.

Yeemee laid a burly arm over the gearshift, put the vehicle back into gear, and drove on without comment.

After nearly an hour of navigating the western fringes of the city, the driver turned left and drove across the open country toward a grove of cottonwoods that marked the course of the Río Grande.

Out of the trees rode the entrepreneur DuRonde, wearing the brown hat and riding the brown horse. He pointed in the direction of the river, and the driver steered the truck as indicated. When the vehicle came to a halt, the man on horseback rode up to the driver's side.

"Who's that?" he asked, without peering in to look closer.

"Just my swamper."

"Well, don't let him get in the way. We've got to get these Celestials across the river. There's Brogan now, ready to take them."

The swamper looked across the river and saw a bearded man, dark-featured beneath a flat brown hat, riding away from a clump of cottonwoods.

"You wait here," said Yeemee, as he killed the engine and heaved himself out of the cab.

The truck rocked and thumped as the live freight unloaded itself, and the swamper watched as the Chinese, carrying the painted artifacts, trudged to the river and into it. The water was suitable for crossing here, for the Chinese went not much deeper than their knees, and then they became taller as they walked out on the other side.

When they had all safely gathered on the American shore, the man called Brogan rode across to the Mexican side of the river. Riding up to DuRonde, he withdrew an envelope and exchanged it for one from the other horseman. The Ramrod

Rider could not hear what was said, but he could see them both nodding. Brogan was smoking a cigar. Yeemee was standing on the ground, apparently listening.

Brogan turned his horse around and re-crossed the river, and as soon as he touched American soil, a detachment of uniformed riders rode out of the trees.

On this side of the river, DuRonde wheeled his horse and was gone in a cloud of dust. Yeemee ran a half dozen steps after him, hollering, and then stopped, shaking his fist and still bellowing.

The Ramrod Rider jumped out of the cab, and as he did so, he saw Ramiro galloping toward him with the dark horse alongside. The Ramrod Rider swung into the saddle, and the chase was on.

Across the flats they pursued the retreating brown horse, which kicked up dust and sped away like a bullet, with the rider crouched low on its back. The two pursuers, likewise, leaned into the chase as their horses' hooves drummed on the hard-baked desert.

The man on the brown horse was headed south and west—away from the river and the town and into the land of rattlesnakes, scorpions, and buzzards. Now the country began to dip and swell, so that the two riders lost sight of their man for short periods of time until they came to a rise again. Then at one point they came to the crest of a hillock, and the man was nowhere to be seen. And his trail, which had been visible up until then, simply disappeared.

Keeping an eye on the far country, the two men rode slowly in widening circles, trying to pick up the trail again.

But no trail could they find; their quarry seemed to have vanished there in the widening desert, where the sun glared down on the scattered rocks and gave them the sheen of a million pieces of silver.

* * * * *

In the days that followed, no new developments took shape. Yeemee, reportedly furious at not being paid, retreated into his house. Whit Whitmore vanished. No one returned to or even visited the DuRonde property.

Ramiro, who had not been paid for his iron work, only smiled. "It is a small price," he said, "to stop a man from dealing with humans as if they were animals."

The Ramrod Rider, who was sitting in La Rosa Blanca with his friends, gazed off in the distance, in the direction taken by the elusive DuRonde. "Yes," he said, taking a drink of ginger ale, "we put him out of business for the time being."

"True," agreed Ramiro as he sipped on his lemonade. "Just for the time being. And even if we had him behind bars, where he belongs, there would be others."

"That's right," said the Ramrod Rider. For in his heart he knew that there would always be men, this one and countless others, seeking wealth at the expense of the human spirit, and for that reason there would always be a need for the Ramrod Rider.

Trouble at Happy Valley Ranch

Of Music and Castles

On the main street of the colorful western town of Durango, Colorado, in the latter part of a summer afternoon many years ago, a lone rider made his appearance. A dark rider was he, on a dark horse, the two moving as one through the shadows cast by the store fronts. Presently there came a gap in the shadows as the horse and rider came to a cross street; and had there been a bystander watching, that person would have seen the sunlight illumine the features of the man, bedecked in black, who called himself the Ramrod Rider.

Down the main street he rode, a wandering knight as always, following the winds of chance. Whence he came and whither he went were dictated by an inner sense, a quiet voice that whispered, "Go thou to that place; thy help will be needed." Thus he traveled, as if guided by an unseen hand, to the places where truth and justice lay close to jeopardy.

An acute observer such as the Ramrod Rider would wonder what danger might lie in hiding at the present moment, for the town of Durango basked in an aura of gaiety. Up and down the main street, sometimes two or three abreast, rode handsomely dressed cowboys who were strumming guitars and singing songs of the open range—for, sooth to say, this was the era of the singing cowboy, who could be found in every nook and cranny of western life.

In addition to the singers and riders, one could see, here and there along the street, trick riders as well as virtuosos of the lariat. Here came a rider executing handstands on the bare back of a galloping steed, while a rope twirler spun out the figure of a dancing girl. Then at full tilt came a thundering white horse, bestridden by a rider dressed all in red satin; the rider shook out a great loop, which grew wider and wider over his head, until he flung it forward and rode his horse right through it!

"That's the Gay Caballero," said a voice. "He shore gets tiresome."

The Ramrod Rider turned in the saddle and beheld a nattily attired cowboy in a high-crowned, cream-colored Stetson, a fringed ivory-colored shirt, and a pair of woolly white angora chaps covering most of his lower body. He was standing on the board sidewalk, with his thumbs hooked in his belt.

His companion, dressed in brown leather chaps and a vest of matching brown leather, a tan shirt, and a flat-crowned, flat-brimmed brown hat, replied, "He's sure stuck on himself."

Then said the first cowboy, "He thinks that horse is a regular Bucephalus, but he'd be nothin' but a puddle jumper next to King Tut."

The Ramrod Rider stopped his horse. "Beg pardon, but did you say 'King Tut'?"

"That's right," said the cowboy dressed in white. "And a mighty fine horse he is. I saw him in Cheyenne a few years back, him and his little lady Bonnie Gray. She jumped him clean over an automobile."

"An open automobile, I'd say," said the cowboy in brown leather.

He of the angora chaps paused in reflection; then he said, "Yes, it had the top down, and Miss Bonnie jumped King Tut across the back seat."

The other cowboy whistled.

The first cowboy regarded the Ramrod Rider and asked, "You new in town, stranger?"

The dark rider, often being a man of few words, merely nodded.

"Well, I'm Chugwater Charlie," said the cowboy, touching the brim of his cream-colored Stetson.

"And I'm Santa Fe Sam," said the other, likewise touching his brown hat.

"And obliged," said the newcomer. "I am the Ramrod Rider."

The other two nodded, as if they had been told the price of coffee had not changed.

"Well," continued the Ramrod Rider, "it's been a pleasure."

Chugwater Charlie held up a clean white hand. "No hurry, my friend. As soon as these other *jongleurs* quiet down, my *compañero* and I are going to sing a couple of songs."

"You won't want to miss it," Sam added. "It will be the world première, right here in Durango."

"Is that right?" queried the rider, uncertain as to what was being heralded.

"Yessir," said Chugwater Charlie. "This will be the first time ever for these songs to be sung in public."

" 'Course," added Sam, "we expect they'll be on the radio in no time at all."

The Ramrod Rider nodded. He had heard radios. "Let me tie up my horse out of the way," he said, "and I'll be back to hear the show."

And a show it turned out to be. Chugwater Charlie and Santa Fe Sam, holding center stage on the board sidewalk, stood facing partially toward one another and partially toward the gathering crowd.

A red ruby ring flashed on Chugwater Charlie's right hand as he gave a few preliminary strums to the guitar strings. Then turning a smile upon the crowd, he said, "This here is Chugwater Charlie's song of romance. I call it 'To the North of Old Cheyenne,' and it goes like this right here." Forthwith he sang the following ballad:

To the North of Old Cheyenne

(Chugwater Charlie's song of romance)

On the plains of wide Wyoming
    To the north of old Cheyenne,
On her homestead on the prairie
    Lives my sweetheart Maryanne.

On a sunny summer morning
    You can see my blue-eyed gal
Out among the cactus blossoms
    On her buckskin horse named Pal.

ADVENTURES OF THE RAMROD RIDER

For she loves to ride the rangeland
    Just as much as any man—
Through the wind and sun and sagebrush
    Of that wide and open land.

I recall the day I left her
    Standing there with reins in hand,
As I left to seek my fortune
    In the world beyond Cheyenne.

With her lower lip a-trembling
    And in each blue eye a tear,
She assured me that she loved me
    And that she would wait one year.

Full of hope and young ambition
    I went out upon the world,
Sure that well within a twelvemonth
    I'd be back to see my girl.

But the world has tricks and teases
    For a lad of twenty-one,
And I soon lost all my money,
    Plus my saddle, horse, and gun.

And I found myself a-groveling
    In a world of men uncouth,
Far away from wide Wyoming

And the pastures of my youth.

Now there's singing in the parlor,
    Jolly songs and bawdy tunes,
As I fill the ladies' glasses
    And I polish the spittoons.

Day by day I hoard my pennies
    As by night I earn my pay,
Hoping soon to have the money
    That will set me on my way.

For the time is drawing nearer,
    As eleven months have passed,
And I long to travel northward
    To my prairie home at last,

Where I hope to be united
    With my sweetheart Maryanne
On the plains of wide Wyoming
    To the north of old Cheyenne.

The balladeer finished his performance with a series of flourishing strums, and then he bowed as the audience broke into applause.

All the while that Chugwater Charlie was delivering his song of romance, his afore-mentioned *compañero* stood quietly with his arms resting on his pendant guitar. When the applause had subsided, he spoke.

"This next song is what some of them there musicologists call a rejoinder. Anyway, it's a response to Chugwater Charlie's song. I just call it 'Down in Santa Fe.' " Then with his guitar swaying as he strummed out the chords, he delivered the following roundelay:

Down in Santa Fe

(Santa Fe Sam's roundelay)

I have seen the blonde-haired lasses
    With their eyes of sparkling blue,
And I've heard the sweet love stories
    Of the brown-haired maidens, too—

But of all the lovely women
    That I've met along the way,
Not a one can match Ramona
    Who lives down in Santa Fe.

With her eyes as black as cherries
    And her lips of ruby red,
And her flowing raven tresses
    Just as soft as satin thread,

She can make my heartbeat quicken
    When she turns her gaze my way,
And I know there's true enchantment
    In the town of Santa Fe.

I recall the day I met her
    On a sunny day in June;
I was sitting in the plaza
    In the early afternoon.

'Midst the tolling of the churchbells
    Calling sinners all to pray,
She came walking through the pigeons
    There in downtown Santa Fe.

In a dark grey dress of cotton,
    And a shawl upon her head,
She had both hands on her prayer book
    And her gaze fixed straight ahead.

Just one look made all the difference
    As she turned and smiled my way,
And I would have died there gladly
    On the ground in Santa Fe,

But my heart went on a-beating
    As the shawl and dress passed by,
And within I felt a summons
    That my soul could not deny.

So I softly rose and followed
    That young woman dressed in grey,
As the churchbells in the plaza

Sang a song for Santa Fe.

At the church I stood and waited
    Till she came back out and smiled,
And I asked if she would like to
    Sit and talk with me a while.

Then began a fond acquaintance
    Which grew stronger by the day.
Now my heart beats for Ramona
    Who lives down in Santa Fe.

A hearty applause greeted this second performer as he closed out his song. In the next moment, the applause renewed itself as the two entertainers swept off their hats and bowed over their guitars. Then, backing away together, they disappeared behind the batwing doors of the Highball Saloon.

The crowd now dispersing, the Ramrod Rider observed a man who had the general appearance of an outsider. He had not been in the audience but rather came walking down the sidewalk to the location of the recent merriment. He wore a grey suit of cotton twill, topped off with a short-brimmed grey hat of the sort worn by traveling archaeologists, or "bug hunters," as field scientists in general were dubbed. Further adding to the scientific image was a full beard, rather neatly trimmed and tended.

The steps of this man tending in the same general direction as the Ramrod Rider's, the circumspect rider let him pass and then fell in behind and stayed at an even distance.

The stranger paused at a corner cigar store, then went inside. The Ramrod Rider, affecting a momentary interest in calabash pipes, likewise went in. Once inside, he noticed that the cigar store served also as an outlet of newspapers, magazines, and books.

The man in the grey suit pawed through the books for a while, and before long he had three in hand. The Ramrod Rider, who had not perused a great many books, could nonetheless read the large print on the spines, and with a glance he absorbed the three titles: *All About Cowboys*, *How to Run a Ranch*, and *Famous Castles of Poland*. Then, glancing furtively, the Ramrod Rider saw the castles of Poland disappear beneath the grey coat.

At this the rider marvelled briefly, learning at once that the distant country had great sights and that someone was willing to steal in order to see them.

Glancing again, the Ramrod Rider perceived that the man in grey now had three books in hand again, but because of the manner by which he now held them, the title of the third book was obscured from view.

With his curiosity thus piqued, the discreet rider lowered his head and looked out from beneath his hatbrim, from which vantage point he was able to observe the grey suit making its way to the counter. Then he heard a voice, one which in the present context seemed disproportionately energetic.

"Oh," said the voice, "I've changed my mind. I think I'll just take these two books after all. I'm sorry for the trouble."

"No trouble at all," said the proprietor.

The Ramrod Rider looked up to see a man with a florid, rotund face and a Teddy Roosevelt mustache. A purveyor of cigars, he was demonstrating pride in his product by inserting a large stogie into his mouth, preparatory to pulling down the handle on the cash register.

The machine clanged and the drawer shot open as the proprietor said, "Two dollars."

The man who looked like a bug hunter already had his hand over the counter, and now he opened it with a flourish and spread two silver dollars on the countertop.

"Just right," said the proprietor, speaking through a rich cloud of smoke which he had just released.

The customer gave a quick laugh, tucked his purchase against his rib cage, nodded, and walked out of the store.

The Ramrod Rider walked up to the counter, so that he might see the title of the book that the stranger had apparently picked up at random and then discarded. In black letters against a pink background appeared the words *Vagile Organisms*, which signified no clear meaning to the informally educated observer.

"How can I help you?" inquired the shopkeeper, who now held out his cigar as if to admire its mashed and soggy end.

"I don't suppose you have any harmonicas," said the rider, cunningly.

"Mouth harps? Nope. Not here. Down the street, though, you'll find any kind you can think of."

The rider glanced again at the pink book, and still making no sense of its title, said, "Thanks."

"Are you a singin' cowboy too?" asked the storekeeper.

"No," replied the rider. "It's for a gift."

"Oh," said the man. "Maybe you'd like to consider some other item. A fine briar pipe, or—"

"For my aging uncle," said the rider. "He doesn't smoke."

"Well, try down the street, then."

The Ramrod Rider thanked the man and left the store. Outside once again, he looked up and down the street. The pageantry of guitar strumming, trick riding, and fancy roping had fallen off somewhat, but the street was far from empty. Finally, as the activity cleared and he could see across the street, he descried the man who looked like a bug hunter, seated on a wooden throne as a bootblack knelt at his feet.

Walking down the block, the stalwart rider crossed the street, then lingered until the man in grey stepped down from his throne, paid the bootblack, and walked away.

The Ramrod Rider looked at his own boots. He had never squandered money on such frivolity before, but he thought he might do so now, as an exercise in reconnaissance.

Thus did he find himself situated on the recently vacated seat.

The bootblack prattled as he went about his work. "Really turned out to be a nice day, considerin' the way things have— but, you know, what with one thing and another, you never know what's goan happen next. After all, the guv'nor says he's not goan raise taxes, and—you know just as well as I do, the guv'nor doan care too much about the workin' man to begin with."

The Ramrod Rider phrased his question artlessly. "Was that the gunder who was sittin' here just before me?"

The bootblack looked up with a broad smile on his pale face. "Oh, no. That's the manager of Happy Valley Ranch." He smiled as he swayed his head back and forth. "Tipped me a dime."

A Paper Cowboy, and Blood From a Turnip

Wondering about the munificence of a man who acquired books by five-finger discount, the Ramrod Rider decided to visit the Happy Valley Ranch and to learn what he might from the lower echelons. Accordingly he found out the way to the ranch, and once there, he went straight to the bunkhouse, where he found an amiable middle-aged man sitting on the steps, engaged in the act of sewing a button onto a set of long underwear.

"Light and set," said the older man.

The rider dismounted and introduced himself. "Name's Tom," he said. "Lookin' fer work."

The other man, whose greying beard was not entirely devoid of tobacco juice, said, "Don't know. You'll have to ask the boss."

"Oh," said the rider. "Where does he keep himself?"

"In the big house. But he just got back from town, and he's in there talkin' with the *segundo*, so I wouldn't be in a hurry if I wanted to talk to him."

"I see," said the rider. Then after a pause he spoke. "What kind of a fella is he?"

"Anybody's guess," said the man.

"Oh?" returned the rider. "What's his name, anyway?"

"Rex Masters," replied the man who was improving the sartorial aspect of his union suit. "And yours?"

"Tom. Like I said."

"Oh, yeah. Well, pleased to meet ya. I'm Gene." The older man smiled, and the Ramrod Rider could see that he was a kindly man.

"Well," said the rider, tentatively, "what is there to know about this fella?"

Gene laughed and gave his visitor a shrewd look. "You want to hear it the way an old coot like me sees it?"

The Ramrod Rider smiled. "You bet."

Gene drew a long breath and let it out. He laid his sewing project in his lap and then began his monologue.

"Well, I'll start at the beginnin', about a year ago, when he first come here. Naturally, everyone in the bunkhouse was interested in what the new boss man was like. When the *segundo* introduced him he said, 'Rex Masters here has just won the Oregon State All-Around Cowboy title.' We all looked at Rex, and he smiled.

"Of course we all noticed his boots. He didn't seem used to 'em. They was brand-new and fit him kind of loose—that was easy to notice, 'cause he has a habit of walkin' back and forth while he talks to all of us at once, and he ain't a short talker.

"Two things about boots—a guy wants to see if they got any stirrup wear, and a guy wants to know if the manure is on the inside or on the outside. You can't know that with a new pair of boots, especially when the fella wearin' 'em comes in from Oregon with a carpet bag full of clothes and his saddle wrapped in canvas.

"Well, after he'd been on the ranch a while, folks notice that saddle. It's new and squeaky, and there on the skirt it has engraved 'Oregon State All-Around Cowboy.'

"Anyway, things go along for a while, and ol' Rex he smiles at everyone. He fires a handful of folks, who don't take it too kindly, and he keeps smilin' at the rest of us.

"Then one day a newspaper man come out to the ranch, and he noticed the saddle. He said, to Rex, 'Where'd you get that saddle?'

"Rex says, 'It was given to me.'

"That's the way Rex talks. Even when he says a lot, he don't tell you much.

"Well, one day as we was workin' the fall roundup, word come driftin' back from Oregon that Rex hadn't earned that title after all. He'd paid his entry fees, but he hadn't gone through with the whole rodeo.

"That brought the newspaper fella right back out. 'What about that saddle?' he asked.

" 'What about it?' Rex says right back.

" 'It says you won the All-Around.'

Then Rex says, " 'I never said I did. I never lied.'

" 'You sure let people have that impression.'

Rex started whinin' then. He said, " 'It's not my fault. I think those hands I laid off are tryin' to smear me in a vindica- tive campaign.'

" 'You mean vindictive?' This reporter was really up on his words.

" 'Yeah,' Rex said. 'That's it.'

"Then the reporter asks him, 'Where'd you get that duster?' You see, Rex has this long linen duster that he wears on occasions, and it has 'All-Around Cowboy' stitched on it.

" 'It was ordered for me,' he said. `I haven't given it much thought.'

" 'But you're not an All-Around?' the reporter asked.

" 'Never said I was,' he says. 'I been real up front about it. I'm just not concerned about titles.'

The newspaper fella said he believed that part, and he went back to town.

"Well, you can imagine how the other cowboys took it. Some said it didn't matter, that that was the kind of thing you could expect out of a boss man anyway. Some said a real All-Around would never do a thing like that. Rex himself sorta dropped out of sight for a few days, and when he come out of hiding, people didn't enjoy lookin' at him.

"I noticed he was partiklerly edgy around a couple of punchers who were real All-Arounds, a couple guys that rattle Mexican and English back and forth. We call 'em Mex and Gringo. They got real names where they come from, of course, which ain't Oregon.

"Then one day Rex says to me, he says, 'Gene, I don't think anyone understands me.'

"What can I say? I'm just the old bunkhouse cook, one of the old-timers, and my word don't count for much. So I just says, 'Myself, I've always saddled my own horses.'

"Rex smiled. He says, 'I bet you have, Gene.'

"I looked at his boots, and I noticed they was still like new. Then I said, 'I think it's too late to ditch that saddle.'

" 'Oh,' he said, 'I've just got to get people to understand me.'

"Then he went back to the big house, and went back to cookin' up more plans for hirin' and firin' people, and it must have made him happy. He was back to smilin' and laughin' in no time at all."

"Well," said the Ramrod Rider, sensing that Gene had come to the end of his narrative, "what kind of cowboy is he, after all?"

"Still hard to say," replied Gene. "They say you don't want to judge a man till you seen him ride."

"And how does he ride?"

"He chokes Lizzie a lot."

The Ramrod Rider understood this figure of speech to mean that the manager of Happy Valley Ranch held onto his saddle horn as he rode. "Some kind of a cowboy," said the rider.

Gene gave a mischievous laugh. "Yeah, but he don't even know the difference."

Regardless of whatever schemes might be afoot in the big house, western hospitality at the bunkhouse level proved true to the code. As the punchers drifted in from their day's work, Gene rustled up a few tin plates of biscuits to go along with a pot of slumgullion.

This stew, as he explained, was like a bank account. "I put in a little bit from time to time, and take some back out, and settle the account at the end of the month."

Seeing the other punchers dig in fearlessly, the Ramrod Rider surmised that none of them had suffered violently from Gene's culinary practices. Therefore, he set to with a spoon, not minding the small details such as the difference between turnip and potato, or between beef and mutton.

After supper, while most of the punchers lounged in the twilight and smoked hand-rolled cigarettes, the Ramrod Rider took it upon himself to go to the big house. Having introduced himself as Tom, looking for work, he set out with that sense of identity.

In another setting, in another time and another place, he might have made the transformation more complete, by donning a set of garments he carried in his saddlebags. Through such a metamorphosis, or retrogradation, really, he would become Tombstone Tom, a pedestrian miner in the trappings of that trade. But arriving on horseback and seeking employment as a cowhand, he found it *apropos* to retain the appearance of what he was—to wit, a rider of the mountains and the plains. But for the sake of simplicity and greater anonymity here at Happy Valley Ranch, he called himself Tom, and came to be known as Tom.

As he approached the big house, he saw a light shining in a front room window. Arriving at an angle more favorable to observation, he saw Rex Masters himself, standing in an oratorical posture. The window being open on this balmy summer's eve, the Ramrod Rider decided to avail himself of the opportunity to improve his understanding of the boss man.

Closer observation revealed that Rex Masters, now hatless, was standing in front of a slate, which was mounted on an easel. With a pointer in his hand, he was tapping from time to time on the slate as an accompaniment to his strident voice.

Further observation revealed that there was one other person in the room—a fat man who could not be very tall, perched on a stool at a distance of ten feet from the slate. The Ramrod Rider surmised that this person must be the *segundo*, or foreman who was second in command. When the bunkhouse hands had been eating their slumgullion chuck, some of them, notably Mex and Gringo, had referred to this person as Gordito.

The voice of the boss man carried on the evening air. "— as part of a new budgeting plan. And just controlling the budget is as important as anything."

"Gotcha." Gordito nodded twice.

"You see, as management, we start with so much per head, for our budget. Then we deduct operating costs, including labor."

"Uh-huh. I follow you."

"We get the owners out here, and we run the same herd past 'em a few times. Old trick, but it works. That bumps up the count."

"Uh-huh."

"And that's the basis for our operating capital. Then we pay the help according to the real head count. So much a head for all the cattle they actually work."

Gordito struck a thoughtful attitude, with his arms folded across the crest of his belly. "But what happens if the owners want to do an audit? You know, another head count later on?"

The maestro's voice softened as he leaned toward Gordito with arms spread out. "There are ways of massaging the figures. For one, we do a head count—actually, we'll call it a census, because if we change the terminology we can make them think in our terms. Anyway, we do the census only during the fall and spring roundups. Explain that it would cost extra to do it any other time."

"I follow you."

"From fall to spring, there's a natural attrition."

"Gotcha. You mean winterkill."

"Yes, but we'll use our terms. Attrition. So, even though these people saw those cattle with their own eyes in the fall, then in the spring they can see clearly that the numbers just aren't there." Masters turned to the slate as he continued speaking. "Let's say we had a ten-percent attrition." The chalk clattered as he wrote on the slate. "We went from five hundred to four-fifty, let's say. Then in the fall, we'll say we had a banner year, show them five hundred and forty head, and claim a twenty percent increase."

"Sure."

"So we ask for a bonus, a bigger budget, and raises in salary."

Gordito's lower lip was pushed out as he leaned forward on his stool, the better to study the slate. "And all this time, we've probably only got four hundred head—or less. We're squeezin' blood from a turnip."

"Sure. But that doesn't matter. It's what we can prove up on paper. And we control the information." Masters made a sweep with the pointer. "Now, follow this. When the numbers go down, we can lay off a few of these peons and tell the rest we've got to pull together to get through the lean times."

"And then we got money to cover our raises, plus some."

"You need to put it in better language. We re-organize, centrally recapture the funds, and then re-allocate."

"I get it, but sooner or later, this place is gonna go broke."

"Of course it will. But by then, you and I'll be out in California, milkin' the real rancho grandy for all it's worth."

"You think so?"

"Watch me."

Counting Empty Graves

Having given a series of raps to the front door of the big house, not once but three times, with intervals of a minute or two in between the percussions, the Ramrod Rider was about to turn away when the door opened. Standing in the doorway, his face in shadow from a chandelier in the background, the boss man looked as if he might have been the master of a dark, secretive castle. The shadowed beard lowered as a nervous, laughing sound crossed the threshold into the evening air.

"Heh-heh-heh-heh-hi-i!!"

"Hello," replied the rider, removing his hat.

"How can I help you?"

"Name's Tom," said the supplicant, in his laconic manner. "Lookin' fer work."

"Great!" cried the boss man, thrusting his hand forward and accepting Tom's. "The *segundo* and I were just talking about a new line of work we wanted to develop. And, Tom, you look as if you're in the right place at the right time!"

Tom nodded.

The master's voice raised in pitch. "You can start in the morning. So you just go on over to the bunkhouse and tell Gene you're one of the family."

Tom nodded again.

The boss man thrust his hand forward again, shook Tom's vigorously, and cried, "Welcome to Happy!" Then he stepped back as the last of his hyena laugh faded in the air between them, and he closed the door of the big house.

With his hat back on his head, the new employee of Happy Valley Ranch walked back to the bunkhouse, where he found Gene setting a batch of dried apples to soak in a pan of water.

"Didja meet the boss man?" he asked.

"Sure did," replied Tom.

"How did it go?"

"He put me on the payroll."

Gene laughed. "You mean he gave you a job."

"Well, yes."

"Could be the same thing. But you always want to count yer change with that feller."

* * * * *

In the morning, Tom received his orders from a man named Brownie. This man, as Tom had been informed by the other hands the night before, had recently risen in status at

Happy Valley Ranch. A few weeks earlier, he had been a lackey who greased wagon axles, rustled firewood for Gene, and looked after the lime supply in the outhouses. Having shown himself to be a company man, he had vaulted over the heads of the other hired hands, figuratively speaking, and now conveyed orders from the *segundo*. Thus did he appear in the bunkhouse in the morning, with something of a swagger, or at least as much of a swagger as he could manage with a low waist and baggy pants.

"Tom," he said, pursing his mouth and bringing his brown mustache into a thoughtful posture, "be ready to go with me in fifteen minutes." Then, as if in afterthought, he added, "Bring your overnight gear. You'll be out for a few days."

On the ride out from headquarters, Tom learned that his new job was to stockpile bones that were scattered in the far reaches of the ranch. He was given to understand that it did not matter if the bones had once belonged to deer, elk, cow, horse, or sheepherder; bones were bones, and Tom was to gather them into piles. He understood that the bones would make their way by wagon into the meadows and pastures closer to headquarters. Brownie intimated that the bones would then reflect a former bovine population at Happy Valley Ranch.

"That way, anyone who's counting can see that they really were here at one time, and they don't have to go all the way out to Hell's Half Acre to see for themselves."

Tom nodded.

They rode on for a few minutes more, and Brownie turned in the saddle. "I could ask you this question," he said. Then, after a pregnant pause, he continued. "How come all you cowpunchers always get on and off on the left side?"

"I dunno," said Tom. "Just the way we learned it."

After an hour's ride, Brownie announced that he had some important things to do back at the ranch, and that Tom could continue west for another mile until he came to a large mountain valley. He was to stay there and gather bones until Brownie came back to tell him otherwise.

Tom nodded and rode on by himself.

Left now to his own devices and no longer feeling the need to project himself into another identity, the Ramrod Rider found his way to the mountain valley, and ere the sun was high he had a heap in the making.

In this manner did he pass the days, hauling bones from the timbered ridges and many-fingered draws, building heaps in the center of the broad valley, and going back out for more. He imagined that other employees, most probably those most loyal to the management, would manipulate the bones into a maximum number of effigies of former occupants of the ranch. In the meanwhile, he thought, he could play along until he found a way to lend a helping hand to the greater cause of truth and justice.

He did not mind the solitude, and he was not averse to passing weathered bones through his hands all day long—nay, to the contrary, there were moments when he thought that handling the bones gave him some link to the creatures that had been, moments in which he felt he was the last to know the subjects before they became converted into things they had never been.

Two weeks passed, and then three, as the rider toiled under the open sky. His ration of hardtack and jerky was running low, and he began to wonder if the management of Happy Valley Ranch had any clear notions of supervision. Realizing then that Rex Masters might be capable of starting a project and then forgetting about it, the Ramrod Rider decided he had better take some initiative; for if he did not, he might dally for too long and thus inadvertently become an accomplice to the scheme he hoped to thwart.

Thus did he decide, on the twenty-second night of his exile, to ride across country to the colorful western town of Durango, Colorado.

* * * * *

Chugwater Charlie and Santa Fe Sam were drinking coffee in the Tip Top Café when the Ramrod Rider tied his horse to the hitching rail in the main street. It was a calm night, with only half a dozen exhibitionists in action, and well past the hour at which a singing cowboy or two might command a crowd.

The Ramrod Rider began by introducing himself and reminding the duo that he had met them on the night of their maiden performance of the songs about Maryanne and Ramona.

"Of course," said Chugwater Charlie. "I remember you. You said you hoped to hear our songs on the radio. Well, it's not far away."

"We've got some big promotions we're workin' on," added Sam. He looked at his *compadre*, who looked back and nodded.

The conversation then fell into such topics as the weather, the uncertainties of the future, and the elusive nature of fame. When the conversation came around to inquiring into the Ramrod Rider's calling, the latter disclosed that he had recently become an employee of the Happy Valley Ranch.

At this news, the two entertainers looked at one another again. Chugwater Charlie said, "We used to work there."

"Till that new fella came along," added Sam. "He gave us our walkin' papers."

The Ramrod Rider allowed that he had heard such a thing and that he had also heard how some malcontent ex-employees had helped circulate the unflattering news that Rex Masters was not the kind of cowboy he had let on.

Chugwater Charlie shook his head. "We didn't do a thing." Then he laughed. " 'Course, if we'd've known, a reporter might've been able to pry it out of us."

Santa Fe Sam yawned and nodded. "It would fall under the category of a good deed."

"Well," said the Ramrod Rider, sensing that he had met some kindred spirits in the realm of truth and justice, "you fellas might be interested in a story." Having engaged the interest of the other two, he forthwith gave a clear and thorough account of the current scheme to bilk the owners of Happy Valley Ranch.

At the end of his story, the Ramrod Rider could see he had ignited some interest in the two musicians. Chugwater Charlie, with his eyebrows raised and his lips pursed, looked at his chum. Santa Fe Sam returned the gesture.

"We do happen to know the owners," said Charlie.

"And they might appreciate a word to the wise," added Sam.

"A good deed," prompted the rider.

"Not to put too fine a point on it," said Chugwater Charlie, "it would be a good piece of work."

The two former employees then asked a few questions of clarification, and the Ramrod Rider could see that they were making sure to acquire an accurate picture of the design.

At length Santa Fe Sam declared, "If we could make a clean sweep of both of them four-flushers, that would be quite the stroke."

"That's right," said Chugwater Charlie. "That Gordito's a bad pill."

"He sure seems to look up to the big boss, though," offered the rider.

"Oh, he might take a leaf from the master's book," said Santa Fe Sam, "but he's not fooled."

"That's right," said Chugwater Charlie as he adjusted the cuff on his left wrist. "No man is a hero to his own valet."

* * * * *

Back to the mountain valley went the Ramrod Rider, still under cover of night but now with improved spirit. He resumed gathering bones, and after another three days of labor, he felt gladdened by the sight of an approaching rider.

As the horse and rider came closer, the gleaner of bones determined that the visitor was not Brownie. This man was larger and sat his horse more awkwardly. Closer still, and a hand wave. Then closer. Then a voice rang out, a voice familiar. It was the voice of the bootblack.

"You must be Tom."

"That I am."

"Well, I come to git you. There's goan be a crew come and pick up these bones, and the *segundo* thought you'd be a good one to drive the wagon."

"Have the axles been greased?" inquired Tom.

"Doan know. But I guess that's somethin' has to be done, you know, before, and of course if it's not one thing it's two, 'cause it seems harder and harder to get anywhere, except in a flivver, maybe, like the one Brownie drives, and you probably have to clean it out, too, but I don't or what you think, maybe you've got your own notions, and if I've—"

"Did you say what your name is?"

"Don't remember if I did or not. But it's Tee Oh Dee."

"That's a queer name," said Tom.

"Ain't it, though? 'Course, it's not too far from Tee Oh Em."

"I suppose," said Tom.

On the way back to the ranch headquarters, T.O.D. rambled on and on, not about the guv'nor but about Rex, and what a fine leader he was, and what great ideas he had for the ranch, and how there were goan be some changes, and even if a man didn't like 'em he had to carry 'em out, because the boss was boss.

When they came to the ridge at the edge of the mountain valley, they paused to let the horses take a breather. The two men turned and looked back at the long, white file of bones that ran through the center of the valley. Outwardly Tom but inwardly himself, the Ramrod Rider realized that those bones would become whatever Rex Masters wanted to make of them, to prove up something on paper.

T.O.D. must have had his own thoughts. With his head cocked almost to his left shoulder, he said, "You know, if you look just right, it looks like somethin' else." Then he frowned. "But I don't know what. Just somethin'."

Dirty Laundry and the Black Bean Revolt

A strange mood seemed to have settled upon Happy Valley Ranch. The Ramrod Rider, still in the demeanor of Tom, sensed a nervous reticence among the punchers as they bellied up to the mess table to partake of Gene's mid-day slumgullion. Few men spoke, and those who did were apt to speak of things far away, such as the Chinaman who ran the laundry in Pagosa Springs, or the lady who operated the Voo-lay-voo Saloon in Ratón, New Mexico.

After the meal had come to an end, Tom helped Gene wash the dishes and thus found an opportunity to ask about the oppressed atmosphere.

"Wal," said Gene, grimacing as he ran a toothpick back into his molars, "it's been gittin' pretty bad these last few weeks, but then this mornin' it took a turn for the worse."

"Oh?"

"You see, they say the boss man has quite a temper, and sometimes you can hear him rampagin' in the big house. Well, somethin' must have touched him off this mornin', 'cause he took his shotgun and killed all ten of my layin' hens. The boys are sorta glum about it because they think it's kinda un-manly of the fella they're supposed to look up to, plus they're gonna miss the eggs."

Tom nodded.

"But like I say, things have been tense." Gene looked around. "I've still got to pluck them ten chickens, and if you give me a hand, I'll tell you the rest of the story."

Thus did the *ci-devant* bone gatherer find himself up to his wrists in a tub of hot water as he re-acquainted himself with the redolence of warm, wet chicken feathers. It occurred to him that Gene had chosen this setting because it was outside, in the open air in front of the bunkhouse, where Gene would be able to see potential eavesdroppers soon enough. As he soused and plucked, the diligent hired hand listened to Gene's narrative. With a glance around, the bunkhouse cook began.

"This story, like the rest of 'em, really begins when the boss man come to the ranch to begin with. You see, he had a little habit that it took people a while to get wind of. That is, he let the dirty laundry pile up.

"Now, I been a ranch hand and a bunkhouse feller since Hector was a pup, and I ain't afraid of dirt or dirty clothes or nothin' like that. In fact, I even wore the same set of long handles all through one hayin' season, even had the upper half tied in balin' twine, so you can't say I'm squeamish. But I draw the line.

"Well, I told you before about how ol' Rex Masters had a little trouble about his All-Around Cowboy saddle. The part I didn't tell is that he had a tendency to let some of his trousers and things get awful dirty, and, as you might expect, he hid the things. Around the bunkhouse everyone knows there's no prospect to lyin' about things like that—you should just clean it up, not throw the dirty laundry in the closet and close the door, like Rex did.

"Well, Rex goes on like nothing happened, even though ever' one knows he's got all this dirty laundry. Then things get a little worse. You know, a lot of the hands were unhappy with the incident about the saddle, and then when he made Brownie into a straw boss, they grumbled even more. It just ain't right to promote someone that don't even know how to cinch up a saddle. I don't need to tell you, but it would do these other jaspers some good to know the code—as long as you ride for the brand, you saddle your own horse, and if you get bucked off, you pull out the cactus needles.

"But anyway, he promoted this Brownie. For quite a little while after that, we didn't see much of Rex. He kept to himself in the big house, workin' out plans, it seemed. He'd come out once in a while, and we'd see what color he'd dyed his beard or how he was combin' his hair. And all the time, we never saw any laundry out on the clothesline. I think you could say he was kinda secret. For example, we never got a straight tally on the fall roundup or the spring roundup either one. And this is a cattle business.

"Then one day a little while back he got us all together and showed us his new plan. He'd changed things around, and he was plannin' to build a lodge so he could run a dude operation. Said he was gonna bring in a lot of outsiders, and it'd be a good business. Then he told us we were all goin' on a trail ride, only we had to go blindfolded and couldn't use a bridle. He called it 'maximizing our potential.'

"Well, we maximized and minimized about it back in the bunkhouse, till finally this one puncher named Gibb, he says, 'Let's take a vote. Everyone gets a black bean and a white bean, and each person puts one bean in the hat. If there's more black beans than white beans in the hat, then we won't ride with this guy.' The talk went on quite a while longer, and then each person got two beans. When it was over, there was more black beans than white ones in the hat.

"Now, newspaper reporters, curious as they are, got interested in the story about the beans. Brownie, of course, he made sure he showed the reporters that he had his black bean left over. Everyone else kept their mouths shut for the time bein', around the reporters, but natcherly amongst themselves they chewed it over pretty good.

"Brownie went around to a lot of the other hands, all worked up, complainin' that everyone was gonna find out about the dirty laundry, now that the reporters was back. Most of the boys looked at it common-sense like. They said someone should wash the laundry, not just keep it all piled up and bustin' out of the closet, stinkin' like it did.

"Maybe that was too reasonable, or maybe some folks are just afraid of how sharp a nose them newspaper people has got. I just don't understand why he keeps the dirty laundry built up. But then again, I don't understand boss men all that good." Gene dunked a chicken into the water, pulled it up dripping, and looked across at his helper. "And I bet you can guess what color bean I got left over."

Tom nodded and dunked the chicken he had been plucking. "How long has this T.O.D. been out here?"

"A little over two weeks," said Gene. "An' he's another one, goes around carryin' orders, while top cowhands are on the end of a pitchfork." Gene snorted. "Now they're gonna start this dude ranch, they say, and that yay-hoo an' Brownie are gonna be the head dude wranglers."

"So they're gonna build a lodge?"

"Yeah. Big one, they say. I don't know where all the money's supposed to come from, but that's the idea. As if he hadn't spent money enough, what with bringin' in painters and carpet-layers and picture hangers to pretty up the big house."

Tom made a long face.

"And you know what?"

"What?" asked Tom.

"I think they've plumb forgot what kind of a business this is supposed to be."

Tom nodded. He plucked thoughtfully for a minute or so before asking his next question. "Why did Rex kill these chickens, anyway?"

"Oh, I think he was just mad at the punchers for takin' the black bean vote, and he knew ever' one was talkin' about the laundry, and he took it all out on these poor biddies." Gene took a look around, then gave his helper a knowing glance, and the conversation subsided.

The helper looked up and saw a horse coming toward the tub and the two men. Atop the horse sat Gordito, with his belly covering the saddle horn. The rider and horse together cast a grotesque shadow, and the horse curled back its upper lip as it approached the mess of feathers and discarded body parts.

"Great job," said the *segundo*. "Doin' a great job!" Then he turned the horse around and rode back toward the big house.

When the *segundo* had ridden out of hearing range, Tom said to Gene, "It was nice of him to tell us that."

"Oh, don't put too much stock in that," replied Gene. "He says the same thing to them two morons."

Of the two morons, the arguably more competent one, Brownie, made an appearance on foot at about the time the chicken-plucking enterprise was coming to a close.

"Tom," he said, pausing as if his having said it carried some importance, "I've got another job for you."

Tom rolled down his sleeves, adjusted his hat, and followed Brownie to a barn on the other side of the big house. Inside the barn, he saw a vast array of harness and tack, feed sacks, dried-up cowhides, canvas scraps, and frayed ropes, interspersed with twists and tangles of barbed wire. Beneath great heaps of the conglomeration sat a four-wheeled ranch wagon.

"We need to straighten out this mess," Brownie said, with his head tipped up as he looked down his mustache at Tom. "Then we got to get this wagon cleaned out so you can use it to haul bones."

"Oh," said Tom, wondering if Brownie had any literal meaning in his use of the pronoun "we."

"So go ahead and get started on it. If you finish before supper, you can ask for me at the big house. I have a meeting with Rex." Brownie gave a nod of authority and then turned around and walked away.

Left now to himself, the Ramrod Rider pondered his work. This seemed to be the style at Happy Valley Ranch, he thought—to leave everything in a big mess and let the next person sort it out. He was on the point of resenting the task when he realized how much worse it might have been. He could have been appointed to work with the dirty laundry.

Flight of the Carpetbaggers

Applying himself assiduously to the task of sorting out the enormous mess, and being left to himself as menial drudges are often left when they are given a disagreeable assignment, the Ramrod Rider pondered all that he had seen and heard of late. That a man like Rex Masters should have so much dirty laundry was not a good sign, nor did it bode well that he sought to maximize the potential of his cowhands by not allowing them to do the real work of their calling.

In the abstract, none of this was new to the Ramrod Rider, for in his wanderings he had encountered other schemers and builders of this caliber—a caliber which, if pressed, he would have described as rimfire rather than center-fire. A grasping manipulator such as Rex Masters, who seemed to have the serviceable talent also of being a shameless (though not barefaced) prevaricator, had little regard for the property or efforts of others. These were such a man's playthings, and if by whim he emptied the coffers of those who trusted him or if by the same or a similar whim he invalidated years of work by trusted employees, he recked naught. So imbued by the opiate of power was such a person, so contemptuous of the subordinates whom he treated as mere chattels, that his glassy gaze was always fixed inward upon his own executive privilege.

Well did the Ramrod Rider know that the rejuvenating West, the portion of our great land that promised freedom and opportunity for the humble and hard-working, had also opened its fields to a thousand varieties of human thistles. So widespread and numerous were these opportunists that even an army of dedicated crusaders could not hope to eradicate them. The best that a single knight errant could wish was to clean up a small patch here and there. Yet he persevered, laboring alone, knowing that his efforts contributed to the sum total of honesty in the world.

Such were the thoughts of the Ramrod Rider, although he did not think in words. He thought in images of light and darkness, of that which was natural and that which was fabricated, of the workers of the world and the overlords who held sway over them. What workers? Those who toiled in the factories and sweatshops of the distant cities, those who bowed to the labor of the hoe in the fields throughout the world, those who helped baby calves find their mothers here at Happy Valley Ranch and throughout the bounteous West. Most of such laborers did not have the freedom to strike on the castle gate, but a fortunate few—who had nothing to lose—could dare to raise a hand against tyranny and duplicity.

By nightfall the Ramrod Rider had worked his way through perhaps a third of the jumbled debris, and with happy thoughts of the prospect of chicken and dumplings, he walked back to the bunkhouse.

"Hello, Tom," said Gene. "Good that you made it. First plate of biscuits is comin' up."

"Could a man guess what's for supper?" inquired Tom.

"No need to guess," said Gene. "It's slumgullion, like always."

"I thought I smelled chicken."

"Might could be," replied Gene. "I had orders to cook up all them chickens and send 'em over to the big house. The nabobs had some kind of commissioners drop in, so there's chicken 'n' dumplin's bein' served, but just not at our table."

"Oh."

"And if you can imagine them two morons sittin' with their napkins tucked into their shirts, pourin' wine and passin' the chicken and actin' like muck-a-mucks, well, then I think you got the picture."

"Nothin' wrong with biscuits and stew," commented Tom.

"And mighty fine," declared Gene, his spirits visibly rising. "Good honest grub for the man that puts in a day's work for a day's pay."

"There's some of us left," said Tom.

"And mighty fine there, too," said Gene, with a wink and a smile. "They're the ones that git the apple pie today."

* * * * *

On the following morning, Brownie seemed pleased to see that his underling Tom had a full day's work to occupy him. "I've got to drive the flivver today," he said, "and I can't be here to show you what to do."

The flivver, as had been explained in the bunkhouse, was an automobile that Rex had purchased with company money. Amidst the discussion, Gene had developed his opinion that the flivver made more sense than a man might expect, what with Brownie not knowing how to saddle a horse, Rex not yet having acquired much stirrup wear on his boots, and Gordito forcing a wheeze out of even the stoutest horses he climbed aboard. While an automobile did not have much use on a ranch, it was just the ticket for bosses who liked to go back and forth from town and who expected to have visitors from afar.

About an hour after Brownie left the barn, the Ramrod Rider heard a sound remotely suggestive of a boy running along a picket fence and clattering a stick against the pickets. Looking out the barn door, he saw a spindly-wheeled automobile leaving the ranch headquarters. Brownie was driving, with his head tilted back and his arm straight out against the steering wheel. He was wearing a short-billed cap. Rex Masters, in the seat next to the driver and attired in his usual grey suit, sported a touring cap and a pair of dust goggles. His rotundity Gordito sat in the middle of the back seat, presumably to keep the vehicle from listing to one side or the other. He was also decked out for the occasion with a pair of goggles, plus a close-fitting canvas cap of the type beloved by sport fishermen. Had the cap been a little closer to green, Gordito might have raised the question of whether there were such a thing as a human frog. Then taking up the rear, sprawled in the rumble seat, was bareheaded T.O.D., who reportedly went along on these excursions because nobody else wanted to crank the engine.

The Ramrod Rider could not help wonder if today's outing had anything to do with the visit of the commissioners the evening before, so at the mid-day meal he kept his ears tuned. As one might expect, the topic came up, and a couple of the more observant punchers confirmed that the commissioners had left the night before, after the wine and wassail. One of those same punchers also reported that Brownie had placed two carpet bags of the valise variety into the automobile, on the floorboard of the back seat. Another puncher observed drily that the nabobs would have needed a couple of steamer trunks to haul off all the dirty laundry, and it was concluded that Rex and the *segundo* had left for a short trip, and perhaps for reasons raised at the meeting of the night before.

Beyond that, the collective knowledge of the ranch hands thinned out and gave way to further speculation, much of which was founded more in jest than in fact. During this time, the junior colleague Tom said little. However, as he returned to his work in the barn and as he labored through the afternoon, he glanced out the open door from time to time to see if anyone was coming back from town.

In the late afternoon he did see a spot in the distance, but before the object on the road had come much closer, the

Ramrod Rider could see that it was not an automobile. A subsequent glance a few minutes later told him it was two men on horseback. A later glance brought more details: a man dressed in white and a man dressed in brown. By then the Ramrod Rider had a hunch, and as the duo rode into the ranch yard, the hunch proved to be correct. The visitors were none other than Chugwater Charlie and Santa Fe Sam.

Immediately the ranch yard was full of Happy Valley Ranch hands, and a hubbub moved among them. It went without saying that if Chugwater Charlie and Santa Fe Sam were here, then the men who had fired them would probably not be back. When the crowd settled down, Chugwater Charlie raised his hand and spoke.

"Boys, we seen a funny thing today, me an' Sam did. We was sittin' in the café next to the railroad station when the train pulled in, and who should come steppin' off the train but a couple of men in flannel suits. They was carryin' leather satchels, and they asked the way to the Happy Valley Ranch. Said they was auditors."

A murmur ran through the crowd, and Chugwater Charlie resumed his oration.

"Now, just about this same time, while the train was still sittin' in the station, an automobile comes puttin' down the street, and who should we see in it, but your friend and mine, in his cap and goggles."

Chugwater Charlie looked over at his *compañero*, Santa Fe Sam, and that worthy took up the thread of the narrative.

"The station master was standin' out on the sidewalk talkin' to these two gents, and when he saw the car come down the street, he pointed at it. Ol' Rex's mouth went wide open, an' he barked somethin' at Brownie, who wheeled the car around and started headin' back out of town. He got to the end of the street, and then he wheeled 'er back around, because by now the men in the flannel suits was runnin' down the sidewalk after 'em."

Santa Fe Sam looked at his fingernails and then continued.

"Well, Rex was still barkin' at Brownie, and they headed right back to the train station, and Brownie slammed 'er to a halt. Then Rex and Gordito piled out, and each of 'em carryin' a carpet bag, they jumped up onto the platform and swung onto the back step of a passenger car as the train pulled out of the station."

A loud cheer went up in the air at Happy Valley Ranch. When order had returned, Chugwater Charlie spoke.

"Now them auditors, they did a little snoopin' around town, and then they checked into the hotel. I reckon after they add up a few figures they'll be out here to tally some more. But from what we heard, it seems the bank account had been pumped pretty dry, and there was a telegram waitin' for Rex at the station. Word was, he had him another job offer."

"Then I bet it wasn't dirty laundry in his carpet bag," called out one puncher. "Like as not, it was greenbacks."

"Could be," responded Santa Fe Sam.

"Where was the telegram from?" asked another puncher.

"California," said Chugwater Charlie. "And they happened to catch the westbound train."

"How 'bout Brownie an' Toady?" called out a cowhand.

"Funny thing," replied Sam. "Brownie had papers for that car in his name, and the last thing we saw, him and his pal was headed down the road to Alamosa."

Not long after they delivered the news, Chugwater Charlie and Santa Fe Sam left for town. Gene pressed them with an invitation to stay for chuck, but they said they had a show to put on that night, and they expected talent scouts to come through town any day now.

Later that evening, while the bunkhouse hands relaxed outside after supper, Gene and his friend Tom washed the dishes.

"Ain't that just the way it goes," said the older man. "They run this place into the ground, sack up what they can, and high-tail it."

Tom nodded.

"Them jaybirds probably got new and better tricks to try where they're goin," said Gene, "but you sure hope some-one'll catch up with 'em in the next place,"

"We can hope so," said the younger man. And then, with eloquence that was rare for him, he said, "And we can also hope that the Happy Valley Ranch can settle down to what it should be doing here in the heart of the golden West: raising cattle."

"You said it," said Gene. "An' I think that's the most I've heard you say since you told me your name was Tom."

The man who had called himself Tom looked around to see if anyone was listening, and then he turned a questioning look at Gene.

The bunkhouse cook regarded him directly. "You're the Ramrod Rider, ain't you?"

"Why, yes, I am," the rider confirmed. "How did you know?"

"I thought so when I first seen you. It's that outfit. I seen it before."

"Really?" responded the rider. "Where?"

Gene smiled. "Long, long ago. My older brother left home when I was just a little pup, but one time he come back to give some money to our dear old mother, and he was dressed like that. He told me he never had hisself a wife nor fam'ly, but just went from place to place tryin' to help folks that was bein' deviled by the big dogs. He said he figgered he'd pass it on to some young fella when he thought he was ready to go to the big roundup." Gene's eyes misted. "I reckon he's gone on, hasn't he?"

"Yes," said the young rider, moved by the emotion of the moment. "But he trusted me to carry on, and God willing, I'll do just that for many a year."

"Well, mighty fine," said Gene.

The rider reflected for a brief moment, and then he said, "I just thought of something."

"What's that?" asked the cook.

"That must make you my Uncle Gene!"

"By golly," said the older man, smiling, "it ciphers that way, don't it?"

"Excuse me," said the Ramrod Rider, who wiped his hands on the dishcloth and went to his bunk. There he took a small package from his traveling bag, and returning to the table where the dishpan sat, he handed the package to Gene. "This is for you, Uncle Gene. I didn't know why at the time, but when I first came to Durango, I bought this."

Gene unwrapped the thin brown paper and revealed a shiny new harmonica. "Why, thankee, boy. I've wanted one of these for a long time." Then the older man's eyes misted again. "I reckon you'll have to be movin' on before long."

"That's right," said the Ramrod Rider. "But you can bet I won't forget my Uncle Gene."

"I know."

With that the two men shook hands—hands that were clean, of course, from the same dishpan.

"I know you helped us out here, boy," said the older man.

"I had to," said the younger man, and he knew he need say no more, for here at Happy Valley Ranch he had found a true kindred spirit who understood the calling of the Ramrod Rider.

Wyoming Welcomes the Ramrod Rider

North to the Double P

Not long ago, a few years after the benevolent administration of our cowboy president Ronald Reagan, a cowboy of lesser renown was on a mission that the venerable cowboy himself, had he known of it, would have applauded. For it was in quest of truth and justice that a black pickup truck made its way north, across the line that separates Colorado from Wyoming, and on to the sandstone bluffs and grassy plains north of Old Cheyenne. A late afternoon summer rainstorm on the high plains had recently ended, leaving the vehicle clean and glossy. Fresh sunlight, which had broken through the clouds to cast a glimmer on the sagebrush and grass, likewise shone through the windshield to play upon the attentive features of the man, bedecked in black, who called himself the Ramrod Rider.

This man, always attentive to the road he was traveling, was at the same time nourishing his sensibilities by playing and replaying, on his cassette player, the melodious strains of "The Streets of Laredo," or, "The Cowboy's Lament." Sadness and beauty poured forth from this moving story of a young cowboy who knew he had done wrong. The Ramrod Rider, himself in the green pastures of youth, had the uncertain feeling, as no doubt did many another young hand, that he had met such a sad cowboy himself.

Enjoy the freshened day as he might, however, the traveler knew that grim business lay ahead. The business had come to him cryptically, at the bucking chutes in Alamosa, Colorado, at a Little Britches rodeo. The Ramrod Rider was helping the younger buckaroos with their bronc saddles when a terse voice behind him muttered, "Message for ya." As he turned to take the message, he saw only the messenger's dove-grey hat brim, slanting down to conceal the person's face as he turned and was gone.

The message, scrawled on the back of an entry form, was as laconic as its carrier. It said, simply, "Puncher needs your help."

Now, as the wandering cowboy drove north toward Chugwater, he wondered again what sort of tight spot had closed around Puncher. The Ramrod Rider had known the cheerful, self-reliant young cowboy for nearly four years, having met him many times at rodeos and livestock shows. He had not been to Puncher's spread, but from the indelible memory of a map that Puncher had drawn in the dust of a Laramie rodeo arena, he knew the ranch was close at hand.

Turning from the main highway to a paved road, thence to a gravel road, and presently from that one to a dirt road, eventually he brought himself to an entryway that typified this part of the country: two upright timbers with a horizontal timber resting on top. The uprights were decorated casually with rusted horseshoes and bleached deer horns while the crossbeam had, branded to it, the interlocking capital P's that denoted Puncher's ranch.

As the Ramrod Rider parked his pickup in the shade of a spreading cottonwood, he saw emerge from the barn a shapely young lady carrying a halter and a lead rope. From the way she buckled the halter and coiled the lead rope, the newcomer deduced that she had just turned loose her horse. As she drew nearer, he saw her wide green eyes, lively and expressive, and he knew that she must be the sister that Puncher had spoken of so fondly.

"Can I help you?"

" 'Magine," he replied, as he stepped out of the cab. "I'm lookin' for Puncher. Friend of his."

She stopped, closed her left hand around the loose end of the rope. "Puncher's not here."

"Out on the range?"

She bit her lip. "Y-yes," she said, with apparent hesitation.

He narrowed his eyes on her. "You sure? I'm a friend of Puncher's, heard he needed help, came as soon as I could."

She must have read the honesty in his earnest face, for she relaxed. She drew the lead rope through her hand, tapped the tasseled end in her open palm. "There's no use trying to hide it. Puncher has been taken to jail."

"To jail! Honest Puncher?"

"Yes, and for a crime he did not commit!"

"I'm sure of that! Hmmm. That means you must be taking care of the place yourself."

"Yes. Daddy . . . err . . ."

"I know, Miss. Puncher told me a while back that your father went on to the big roundup."

She broke into a sob. "Yes. First Momma, then Daddy. And now Puncher is locked up, and I'm left here to run the ranch all by myself. It seems like—everything— is—just—" And here she broke into a series of faltering sobs.

"Don't worry," said the rider, as he drew her to him with his protective instinct. He patted the back of her head, gently, as she bedewed his black shirt with tears. "Don't worry. I am the Ramrod Rider. I am here to help you."

* * * * *

Over lemonade, the green-eyed prairie princess told her visitor of recent occurrences. "It all started when a rich man from Denver bought the old Leaning Wye, to the south. He started bringing in a lot of equipment, and padlocking gates. We came up short a couple of two-year-old steers and then a yearling heifer. When Puncher asked him about it, he became belligerent. He said they had no beef on the place, that he was developing the natural gas underground, and that Puncher and I should mind our own business. Puncher had me quit riding the fence lines next to his."

"What's this Denver fellow's name?"

"Daniel Durant."

"Daniel Durant. Hmmm." Deep in the pools of the Ramrod Rider's memory there was a faint ripple, but nothing came to the surface. "Somethin' about that name. Oh, well, maybe it'll come to me. What happened next?"

"The next thing we noticed was that our barn down on Dry Creek had been pushed over."

"Pushed over? Flat?"

"No, just rammed into with some large piece of equipment—Puncher showed me the tracks—so that it stands all tilted and leaning. Puncher was getting ready to go to work trying to straighten it up when they took him to town."

"What did they haul him in on?"

"Mr. Durant accused him of stealing a large piece of equipment—he said Puncher was trying to knock over the building for the insurance money, and then blame it on Mr. Durant."

"I'd like to look at that barn. When can we head down that way?"

"It's just a little late in the day for it now. I'd say first thing in the morning. You *are* staying around, aren't you?"

"Got to," he said. Pursing his lips and then licking them, he continued. "What do you think if I put up in the bunkhouse, then, Miss —?"

"Oh, dear me. We haven't even introduced ourselves. My name is Penelope Pendergast, but my daddy and my brother called me Puss. Most people call me Penny. You can call me either one." She smiled.

"Mighty fine, Miss Penny."

"Just 'Penny' is good enough. And did you tell me your name, out in the driveway?"

"I am the Ramrod Rider," he replied.

"That's an unusual name. Is there a story behind it?"

"A short one," he returned, glancing at the clock. "Probably take me one tall glass of lemonade to tell it." He helped himself to another glassful, as his hostess opened the kitchen window to let in the cool of the evening.

"I had a name once," he began, "and probably a family, but I suffered what you might call a loss of memory. One hot afternoon I came to in the middle of a rodeo arena, with my crumpled hat next to me, my mouth full of dirt, and my mind empty of all details except that I had been riding a horse named Buttermilk. I heard the announcer say, 'Looks like he'll be all right. Give him a hand, folks, because that's all that cowboy's takin' home!' I realized that it didn't matter whether I could remember my name, because I wasn't going to the pay window anyway.

"I was still empty-headed when I got back behind the bucking chutes, and I met an older fellow dressed in black like I am now. When he found out that I had no idea of where my wallet was, or where my vehicle was (if I'd even had one), he took me in. I didn't have so much as a pair of initials on my chaps to give me a hint. After two days I still didn't know who I was, and the oddest thing was, I wasn't very worried about it.

"On the third day, the old man asked me what I had in mind to do. I told him that my mind was a blank slate, and I could start a new life if I wanted. His face crinkled and his eyes softened, and he said 'I might have one for you.'

"He gave me a trunk, which is now locked in the canopy of my pickup. In the trunk was a pair of revolvers on a gunbelt, a set of saddlebags, and several black bandanas, shirts, and trousers. The clothes fit me mighty fine. I gave my old clothes, my riding chaps, and my bronc saddle (he had helped me get it back from Buttermilk) to a benefit sale for an orphanage, and I joined him."

"Excuse me for interrupting," Penny broke in, "but how long ago was this?"

"It's been seven years," replied the rider. He took a drink of lemonade and resumed his story. "Over our campfire, he told me he had been taken in, as an orphan, by a man in black. The man had raised him in a cave, had taught him to be brave and to love truth and justice. One day the man in black returned to the cave, all shot up, with just enough life in him to pass on the calling of the Ramrod Rider. The young man accepted.

"For nearly fifty years he answered that call, and now, as he put it, the time had come for him to cash in his chips. He said he was glad I could sit in for him and take cards. Not long after that, he crossed the Great Divide.

"And so," he concluded, "I am not the first to be called the Ramrod Rider, and, God willing, not the last."

His hand was halfway to the table, setting down the lemonade glass, when he heard a twig snap outside, followed by hurried, retreating footsteps. Lurching to the door, he peered out into the moonless evening. He turned to look at Penny.

"I'd better check on my gear," he stated.

Despite the gathering darkness, he was able to determine that no forced entry had been made into the locked aluminum canopy of his pickup. Beyond that, he could only surmise that some drifter of the night had heard all or part of his story. Well—no matter; he was here to help Puncher (and now Puss, or Penny), not to protect his own career or the curtained past beyond it. He went back into the ranch house.

"That's the way it's been of late," said Penny. "I always feel as if someone is watching and eavesdropping. Daddy would be dismayed to know that we sleep with the doors locked." She paused, eyelids lowered, then looked up. "I'd feel safer if you slept in the house."

"Reckon I can bunk in Puncher's room."

"Down the hall on the right," she said, with an audible tone of relief, as she pointed with her hand, palm upward and relaxed.

That night, as the Ramrod Rider lay with his sleepless head upon the pillow, he was imbued with a sense of purpose: to uncover the murky designs of this Daniel Durant, to help clear Puncher's name, and in the meanwhile to protect the rancher's daughter, brave Puncher's green-eyed sister, who lived on the grassy plain.

Ridin' for the Double P

Having ridden on horseback, in the company of pretty Penny, to the imperiled barn on Dry Creek, the Ramrod Rider determined that it might be brought erect again through the employment of a large turnbuckle and appurtenant cables. Fortunately, the patriarch of the Double P, Preston Pendergast, had possessed a prodigious turnbuckle in the days of Puss and Puncher's childhood. After ransacking her memory and then the loft of the barn at headquarters, the rancher's winsome daughter located the item in question. Agreeing with the

Ramrod Rider that it was "just the cat's whisker" for the job, and noticing with him that they would still need auxiliary cables, she offered to go to town. She added, almost parenthetically, that she needed a few items for the kitchen anyway, such as bacon, flour, and lemons.

The Ramrod Rider saw, at this time, the opportunity to ride the fence lines. Glancing at a map of the ranch and thereby fixing in his mind a comprehensive picture of its metes and bounds, he re-saddled the buckskin gelding he had ridden earlier. Tying on a saddlebag with a few fence repair items, he was in the saddle before the dust had settled from Penny's departure.

Following a fenceline, he struck southward, at ease to be in the saddle again but always watchful of the terrain around him. Twice he dismounted for minor repairs on the fence, and his mission took him through an open gate and into a larger pasture. He followed the fence as it continued south by southeast, and before long he was swallowed by a sea of billowy grassland. Not a tree or building could be seen, and only distantly a windmill. Tying him to the reality of this time and place was the fence along which he rode, a line that led backwards to ranch headquarters and forward to the end of the Double P. The fence seemed less and less to be a boundary and more and more to be a line across a vast and boundless solitude.

Suddenly he became aware of a fellow creature, for his horse pricked up its ears and looked toward the southwest, where, standing white and tan in the prairie sun, could be seen a buck antelope. This kindred spirit watched curiously as the rider nudged the buckskin back into motion. Then the antelope flashed its white rump and broke into a run, wheeling and zig-zagging, as if to invite his new companions to play. The Ramrod Rider, entranced by and immersed in the primordial setting, gave free rein to the buckskin, which broke into a gallop. Gradually the horse gained on the antelope, cutting a diagonal, as it were, through the zig-zag course of the fleet pronghorn.

Out of sight was the fence, out of sight was the windmill, to the effect that the rider felt cut free, adrift on the ocean, innocent of the world that might lie beyond those distant shores, innocent of the differences that might separate him from the earlier wearers of the timeless black garb, this cloak of identity that, as the prairie grass blurred beneath the drumming horse hooves, took him back to the cave and merged him as one with those earlier men, one man now, now as before, the man bedecked in black, who called himself the Ramrod Rider!

Then the antelope was gone, like a duck under water, and the horse jolted to a walk. The sight of a metal building in the distance brought the rider back to a sense of the here and now. He was riding for the Double P, it was nearly summer in wide Wyoming, and somewhere nearby a man named Daniel Durant was up to no good.

Topping a rise to the left, he scanned the country that he had loosed himself into. Off to the east, still slanting south-ward, was the fence he had left. Now to the north and west lay the windmill. In his mind's eye he pictured himself to be at the south end of the Double P, five miles from the house and three miles from the point where he left the fence. Yon metal building, he reasoned, would be on the Leaning Wye, and thus an item of interest.

As he drew near to the building, he recognized it as the type of edifice often constructed at field sites on oil and natural gas operations. If Daniel Durant were indeed developing energy resources, such a building would be expected. But if so, why the diversion of attention to the barn at Dry Creek, now some miles to the north and west?

Pondering these questions, the Ramrod Rider hitched the buckskin to the fence, for, finding no gate, he resolved to climb through the fence and approach the building on foot. This he did, noticing as he drew closer that a road, or more accurately a dirt lane, had been worn into the prairie on the opposite side of the building. The rider divined that the road led to a door, and thus he approached what would be the rear of the building.

Rounding the corner of the building, which from a distance looked like a shed but proved to be the size of a barn, he was met by two men, one tall and one short. The ensuing tumult consisted of a *mélange* of impressions: a driving fist into his stomach, the smell of chewing tobacco, the loss of balance as he fell backwards, looking into two unshaven faces shaded by a sunny blue sky beyond. A boot in the stomach, driving out the rest of his wind. Then a blow to the back of the head that dimmed all the lights.

Some time later, with his hat jammed onto his head, he was being dragged backwards by two men, one tall and one short, who pulled him by the armpits and left his bootheels dragging in the dirt. It was drag and stop, drag and stop, drag and stop, then the creak of fence wire and the milling of a horse. He was swaying and lurching, couldn't get his feet on solid ground. Then he found the horse's neck, followed the reins to where they were tied around the saddle horn. He was in the saddle. That was it. His hands found the horn as his feet found the stirrups. A man had to hang on. A good horse would take him home through a blizzard. Must be a storm, he couldn't see a thing. Warm rain pattered on his hands, his hat brim, his eyelids. No wonder it was so dark. He couldn't get his eyes open. The good horse would take him. A man had to hang on.

Twin Revelations

The Ramrod Rider opened his eyes at last, blinking away water. He heard the clank of a bucket handle and then a voice.

"I think he's coming to."

Turning his head to one side, he perceived the buckskin, reins trailing, cropping the ranch house lawn.

"Look up at us here, pardner," the voice said.

Endeavoring to look up, the beleaguered rider could not seem to focus his vision, for there was a buxom, blue-eyed cowgirl standing next to herself. He blinked his eyes, but still he saw two of her. "Who are you?" he asked.

"I'm Wyoma . . ."

"And I'm Wynema," said the voice.

He propped himself up by the elbows, squinted his eyes closed, and opened them again. He looked to his left. One horse. He looked ahead. Two cowgirls. "How did you get here?" he asked.

"In that pickup," said the voice.

Looking to his right, he perceived a single red pickup, a Dodge, with dual rear tires. "Both of you?" he asked, cunning-ly.

"Of course," said the voice.

"Could you help me up, please?"

"Sure thing," said the voice.

The cowgirl divided more clearly into two. One of her took his left hand and the other of her took his right hand. They helped him up. Standing between them, like the O between the two D's on the hood of their pickup, he said, "Thank you, ladies."

"Are you all right?" they asked together.

"I think so," he replied, rubbing his head.

"You look like you been rode hard . . ."

". . . and put away wet," they said.

"Did it rain?" he asked.

"Just a little sprinkle . . ."

". . . about an hour ago."

"I thought so. I was on that horse. Ridin' the fence lines. Two men roughed me up and left me kinda groggy, then put me back on the horse. He took me home." He saw curiosity in both pairs of blue eyes. "I'm here to help out. Friend of Puncher's."

"Oh."

"Are you friends of Miss . . . Pendergast?"

"You bet. We rodeo with her . . ."

". . . and we team rope on our own."

"Maybe you can tell me about these two hombres that jumped me. I happened to be across the fence on Daniel Durant's place, and these two hands, one tall and one short, changed my tune for me. You know these fellers, both kinda dirty and not real friendly with a razor?"

"Sounds like Laramie Larry . . ."

". . . and Cheyenne Charlie."

"Not rodeo hands, are they?"

"No, just two-bit roughnecks . . ."

". . . who came to work for Mr. Durant."

"That figgers. An honest cowboy would've given me a man-to-man chance. By the way, which is which?"

"Laramie Larry is the lean one . . ."

". . . and Cheyenne Charlie is the chunky one."

"No, I mean you two. Which is which?"

"I'm Wyoma . . ."

". . . and I'm Wynema."

"Well, I'm mighty glad to meet you both."

It would be difficult to determine how their conversation might have continued, for at this juncture a crunch of gravel announced the return of the mistress of the Double P. After greeting her friends and hearing of the Ramrod Rider's mishap, she proposed that they all work together to straighten up the barn on Dry Creek, after having first repaired to the ranch house for lunch.

The Ramrod Rider was much assisted by the twin cow-girls and their friend, whom they alternately called Penny and Puss, to the Ramrod Rider's continued consternation. Nevertheless, their assistance was quite invaluable. Wyoma, standing on Wynema's shoulders, secured a cable to the upper northeast corner of the barn while Penny snugged the other cable to the lower southwest corner; the Ramrod Rider, meanwhile, held up the bulky turnbuckle until the cables were secure. Then, he applied his muscles to the task of turning the device, which exertion began to return the edifice to a semblance of its former rectitude. The jubilant crew left the turnbuckle and cables attached, until such time as the barn could be braced with planks and nails.

Upon completion of this first phase of the task, it was disclosed that the twin cowgirls had come, originally, to invite their friend to join them for an evening session of tying goats. The Ramrod Rider, cognizant that he would be left to his own designs, announced his intention to gather more impressions of the Durant enterprise.

"Before you go," said Penny, "I should tell you what I heard in town, though I don't know what to make of it."

The rider perked his attention, and he saw Wyoma and Wynema do likewise.

"Mr. Durant has a visitor," Penny continued, "a surgeon who is reported to be one of the nation's leaders in organ transplants."

The twins looked at each other in wonderment.

"And I also heard that Ollie Oddjob has gone to work for him."

"Ollie Oddjob?" queried the twins, with matched disgust on their faces.

"Who's he?" inquired the rider.

"Just a shiftless bum around town," replied his hostess. "If he ever works at all, he works as a short-order cook."

"Makes me wonder," said the rider, "what a man in the natural gas business is doing with a heart surgeon and a fry cook."

* * * * *

The day was hastening to its decline, or, as it is said on a different ocean, the sun was slipping over the yardarm, when the Ramrod Rider embarked again on a journey through the crests and swells of prairie sea. The crepuscular tones of sunset played upon the grass and sage, creating a muted iridescence through which the Ramrod Rider rode in wonder.

He arrived at the boundary fence as nightfall gathered. Knowing that there was neither cattle commerce nor cowboys at the metal building, he had minimal fears that the buckskin would find equine cousins with which to nicker back and forth. Nevertheless, he laid a palm over the horse's nostrils, by way of parting admonition.

Even from the fence the rider could see light emanating from windows on either side of the building. As he approached, he realized that the light came from ground level windows, as from a basement, as well as from standard height windows. He was pleased to reflect that the light would hinder the assailant thugs from approaching in the dark; likewise, he took caution from the thought that he would be easily discernible in the light. Thus, he resolved to keep in shadow as best he could.

Deciding to start from the bottom and work up, he flattened himself next to the building and peeked into the basement, where he expected to see machines, pipes, tanks, gauges, and the sort of equipment involved in exploiting natural gas reserves. To his surprise, he saw a row of stainless steel cages, each holding a large simian creature. As the Ramrod Rider pondered with himself whether he should think of the animals as monkeys or as apes, he saw two men step into view. They were looking at the captive animals.

The human on the left was a dapper man of middle height, dressed in grey suit and tie with a matching homburg hat. He wore wire-rimmed spectacles and a grey Vandyke beard. This must be the doctor, decided the Ramrod Rider, who then turned his attention to the other man.

This man, somewhat taller and heavier than the other one, but younger, had greying blond hair that had thinned extensively on top, a condition made more prominent because of the overhead lighting and the Ramrod Rider's vantage point. As the larger man turned to smile at his interlocutor, he brought into view an impassive brow and prominent cheekbones, the latter a mixture of Mongolian fierceness and Irish blush.

Both men were drinking red wine from stemmed glasses. The larger man, whom the vigilant rider took to be none other than Daniel Durant, displayed an emptied wine glass as he arched his brows. The dignified man nodded, and they moved from view. From the elevating gaze of one of the apes, the rider inferred that the men were going upstairs. Then the light went out.

The Ramrod Rider took this opportunity to glance into the main floor of the building. Here he experienced a sensation that matched his surprise of a few minutes earlier, for the inside of the building held a full facsimile of a truck-stop diner, complete with tables, counter, stools (with metal pedestals), coffee urns, display cases with fruit and cream pies, a pass-through service window, and beyond that, a greasy, smoky kitchen. The cooking area was inhabited by a slovenly-looking man of un-athletic build, stoop-shouldered with a paunchy belly, tattoos crawling out from beneath the sleeves of a soiled T-shirt, cigarette dangling from the lips, stubble of beard on sagging cheeks and unfirm chin, and dark, unwashed hair slicked back and held by the grace of either pomade or bacon grease. This was no doubt Ollie Oddjob, Daniel Durant's lackey, currently engaged in the act of cooking hamburgers on an immense, smoky griddle.

Now the observer saw, seated at the counter, the two ruffians from earlier in the day. They were drinking coffee and smoking cigarettes. Here and there at the tables were seated half a dozen other men, all of the same ilk as those at the counter—unwashed, indolent, well-fed, and probably ill-mannered. A quick study told the rider that none of them looked like ranch hands or like regularly employed hands of any sort. A man who works, as the rider well knew, carries the marks of his work in the form of wear, tear, dirt, and smudge. These men, by contrast, were the sort of chronically unemployed or minimally employed men who were never honestly dirty or freshly scrubbed. Their type he knew, but other questions remained unanswered: why were they here, and why was Ollie Oddjob cooking hamburgers for them?

The Ramrod Rider formed these questions after only a minute or two of sharp observation, at the close of which time a light flicked on in the forepart of the building. Durant and the doctor, no doubt. Upon hearing a window slide open, the stealthy rider crept to the edge of the window and lent an ear.

He heard the clink and splash of wine being poured, and then a voice.

"Well, Dr. Hackmesser, what do you think of my set-up?"

"The baboons look as if they are excellent specimens."

"How long do you think it will be until I can market them?"

"Right now there is a recession in that market, but I am certain it will pick up. There are thousands of babies out there with defective hearts, and not many donors. One more transplantation, even marginally successful, once it hits the news, will open the market for as many baboons as a small-time supplier such as yourself can provide."

"I see. And what do you think of my other . . . specimens?"

"Quite frankly, Mr. Durant, I am of a mixed opinion regarding your, shall we say, low socio-economic humans."

"Indeed? I'm interested in knowing more."

"On one hand, they all look sturdy and indestructible."

"Yes . . ."

"But on the other hand, I would think that you might have some . . . sleeker-looking specimens, showing more evidence of exercise and healthy diet."

"I have given it some thought, doctor."

"No doubt you have, and I am likewise interested in your viewpoint."

"Let us look at it this way. Dr Hackmesser, what is the usual physical condition of your clients—er, patients?"

"It's always hazardous to generalize, of course."

"Of course."

"But the typical recipient is middle-aged or older, over-weight, under-exercised, and quite likely troubled by smoking, drinking, and poor eating habits."

"With that profile in mind, doctor, I have reasoned as follows. The ideal organ, it would seem, would be from a donor who is well exercised and scrupulously dieted. However, such an organ, when introduced to the hostile environment, often fails to cope with such a combination of systemic stresses."

"Certainly."

"It stands to reason, then, that an organ that is not a stranger to such abuses, but rather has proven to be quite durable in response, might have more immunity when it is introduced into the new, and shall we say, vile, environment."

"That is one line of reasoning, Mr. Durant, and not necessarily an erroneous one."

"Worth trying, at least a few times, in the interests of science and finance?"

"In the interests of science and finance," affirmed the doctor.

There followed a clink of glasses and then a silence, during which time the Ramrod Rider felt a strain in his interior, as if his own organs were groaning in dismay and apprehension.

He tried to solace himself with the thought that he was well exercised and reasonably dieted, but the anxiety beneath his ribs prevailed. He looked in through the window just long enough to see Durant and the doctor holding their wine glasses aloft, by the stems, as if to search for impurities in the wine. Then it was to horse and away for the Ramrod Rider.

Tensleep Tom Takes a Hand in the Game

In the morning, after having related his strange findings to the mistress of the Double P, the Ramrod Rider announced his intention to check on the barn at Dry Creek and to look over the countryside. "I can scout out the country from Dry Creek to the Leanin' Wye," he said, "and look at things from that angle." Without further ado, he saddled the buckskin and was gone.

Upon approaching the barn, the rider derived the impression that the building still had a lean to it and that it might benefit from a few turns on the prodigious turnbuckle. This task he performed to his satisfaction; then he resumed his morning ride.

Following the dim impressions made some time before as the heavy equipment had moved across the prairie, the Ramrod Rider found himself again headed in the direction of Durant's holdings. He came, at length, to a place where the fence had been broken down. He urged his mount across, resolving to repair the fence upon his return.

"Must be on the Leanin' Wye by now," he said to himself.

The trail led him further south, for perhaps another mile, until, topping a rise, he came upon a ramshackle barn nestled down in a sheltered vale. The tire tracks led to the barn; away from the barn, in the direction of the truck stop diner, stretched a dirt road that had seen recent wear.

Dismounting and then leading the horse, the rider approached the barn, the door of which was hanging crooked and unlatched. It creaked as he opened it, and the morning sun shed light upon recent questions. Parked in the barn was an industrial-sized tractor, facing the door, with its front-loading bucket raised high in the air. Suspended from the bucket was a chain, a block and tackle, and a crossbar or gambrel, used for suspending slaughtered animals. A heap of cowhides, one with the Double P brand visible, completed the story.

"Hold it right there," a voice behind him rasped. Then he heard the clickety-snick of a rifle. He turned to look into the muzzle of a well-oiled Winchester, held firmly in the grasp of Cheyenne Charlie, who answered, "You don't learn very good, do you?"

Laramie Larry emerged from the darker recesses of the barn, carrying a rope. "We got just the method fer coolin' down hotshots like you," he taunted, fastening a loop around the Ramrod Rider's torso and arms. He jerked the reins from the rider's hand, slapped the horse on the rump, and hollered, "Hee-yah! Git away from here."

The Ramrod Rider struggled instinctively, endeavoring to loosen the bond that held him. Then the Winchester barrel came down upon his head, and he saw a brief shower of exploding lights.

* * * * *

When he awoke, he was very cold. Feeling around, he determined he was on a concrete floor. Reaching out, he found a wall. Pulling himself uncertainly to his feet and following the wall, he found a light switch. Dark became brilliant light. A quick glance told him he was in a walk-in cooler, and his companions were hanging quarters of Double P beef.

Pushing the latch on the door, ever so slowly and quietly, he disengaged the device and opened the door a crack. At a distance of fifteen feet he saw a metal cage, and he knew himself to be in the baboon basement. He shivered as he thought of the common fate of the animals in back of him and the animals in front of him, a fate that could, without too great a stretch of the imagination, be his.

Slowly he opened the door again and, seeing no one on guard, deduced that the door at the top of the stairs must be locked. Looking upward at a window behind him, the window through which he must have peered on the evening previous, he saw the lower half of a man's body slouched against the building.

"Probably asleep," muttered the Ramrod Rider. Keeping out of sight nevertheless, he took a full measure of the room. There were only two windows, one that was guarded and one that was inside the baboon cage, the steel slats of which ran from floor to ceiling.

After some cajoling and cavorting, the Ramrod Rider induced the baboon to leave the cage. Then, grabbing two milk crates he had appropriated for the occasion, he closed himself into the pen, positioned the crates under the window, and with the work of a moment was a free man again.

* * * * *

Back at the ranch, the Ramrod Rider divulged his plan to Puncher's green-eyed sister, who listened attentively.

"I'm not having any luck going through the back door, so I'll march right up to the front door. Then we'll blow this case wide open."

"But they know you now."

"I've got a disguise in my saddlebags. That, and a different horse, and I'll be a stranger again."

In a matter of minutes the Ramrod Rider was metamorphosed, by the help of loose-fitting garments and a set of mustachios, into the perfect picture of an itinerant ranch hand.

"Whaddya think?" he queried. "Do I look like the gen-u-wine article?"

"You sure do," replied Penny. "Now, tell me what you want me to do."

"Gimme about an hour's start, and then fetch the sheriff and—yep, them two cowgirl friends of yours. They seem pretty handy."

"You're even talking differently," she marveled.

"Good," he said, in his usual voice. "This has to be perfect."

"What do you call yourself?" asked Penny.

"Waal," he drawled, "Down in Arizony I went by Tombstone Tom. Up here, I reckon I better be . . . Tensleep Tom. Whaddya think?" He paused with his hand on the doorknob.

"It's perfect, sure enough," she replied, her green eyes brimming with admiration. Then she stepped toward him quickly, kissed him on the cheek, and said, "Good luck, Tom."

Thus it came to pass that the Ramrod Rider, recently y-clept Tensleep Tom, rode a sorrel mare up to the front door of Daniel Durant's establishment. As Cheyenne Charlie was still asleep at the side of the building with his rifle barrel jammed in the dirt, the rider inferred that there was still a baboon running loose in the basement.

The denizens of the diner all looked up as Tensleep Tom walked in.

"Can I help you?" asked the cook, who looked no better by the light of day.

"Lookin' fer Mr. Durant."

"He's not here. I'm Ollie, the bunkhouse cook. This here's the bunkhouse, as you can see."

Tensleep Tom looked around. "Kind of a funny-lookin' bunkhouse to me."

"It's Mr. Durant's idea. What d'ya want to talk to him about?"

"Lookin' fer work. Heard he just bought this place, thought he might need another hand."

The cook looked him over. "You look like the kind of man he might have some use for. You want a hamburger?"

"Sounds mighty fine to me."

"Lemme run downstairs and get another pan of meat. I got a whole batch I just ground up last night. It's in the cooler."

Tensleep Tom held up his hand. "Don't bother just fer me. I can wait till the others eat." He pulled a chair around and sat straddling it, resting his forearms on the chair's back. "Why don'tcha tell me about the kind of work I might get into here?"

Ollie Oddjob sat down as he fished a cigarette from his apron pocket and lit it. "Reg-lar stuff," he said, evasively. "You know, cowboyin' and such."

"Hope he don't want me to work with no shovel."

"I can't say, mister."

"Call me Tom. Tensleep Tom."

"Like I say, Tom, I can't say. But you look like his kinda man. Work's kinda slow right now, but he's keepin' all these fellers on the payroll till work starts up."

"Feeds 'em good?"

"You bet. I'm the cook."

"Uh-huh. Sounds like a good man to work fer." Tensleep Tom sniffed his mustachios.

"No complaints so far," said the cook. "This ain't the Di-amond Horseshoe, you know, with candle operas on the tables and waiters speakin' French, no, ner any desk clerks and room service valleys..."

At that moment a vehicle door closed, and all eyes turned to the front door. It opened as Daniel Durant walked briskly in, jingling his keys.

"I need four men," he said.

No one stirred.

"I need four men right away," he emphasized, and then pointing at those sitting closest, he said, "you, you, you, and you. Go get in the back of the pickup." As the men arose reluctantly from their tables, Durant turned to his cook. "Ollie, whose horse is that?"

"This feller here."

Tensleep Tom pushed himself up from his chair and looked into the steely blue eyes of Daniel Durant. "Name's Tensleep Tom. Lookin' fer work."

Durant took his hand in a vise-like grip and released it. "Very well."

The cook spoke up. "You need a feller like him this afternoon, Mr. Durant?"

The blue eyes looked up and down at Tensleep Tom, who stood with his thumbs in his belt. "Let's make sure we feed him first, Ollie, before we put him to work. These other four men will do just fine." He and the cook exchanged nods, and Durant turned to Tom. "You're welcome to stay on, mister. I might have something for you in a day or two."

"Obliged," said Tensleep Tom, as Durant left the room.

Ollie Oddjob sat down and lit another cigarette. He said to Tensleep Tom, who also sat down, "I hope you like hamburgers and French fries. That's what's fer supper."

"Love 'em."

"Good. That's what we have every day. Sometimes fer variety we have steak and French fries, or hamburgers and hash browns."

"Uh-huh."

"Haven't had steak and hash browns yet, though. That'd be good fer a change." He smoked thoughtfully.

"Sounds mighty fine." Tensleep Tom sniffed his mustachios again.

Suddenly Laramie Larry burst into the room. "Holy smokes!" he declared. "There's a truckload of dames comin' down the road."

Ollie Oddjob grinned.

"Don't sit there like a dummy," said the lean roughneck. "There's a sheriff followin' em!"

Ollie looked at Larry and then at Tom. "Mister, you better get down in the basement."

"I got no trouble with the law," said Tom.

The other two idle men, who had been sitting by, slinked out the front door. Ollie looked at Larry, Larry looked at Tom, and Tom looked at his boots. They were the Ramrod Rider's boots, a detail that made Tensleep Tom uneasy. He looked up to find Laramie Larry studying him. "What's yer name, mister?"

"Tensleep Tom."

"You remind me of a galoot we caught snoopin' around here, only you don't seem as stupid as him."

"Is that right," countered Tensleep.

"You bet it is," scowled Laramie Larry, producing a pistol, "and I bet you and him would make good company. Ollie, let's show this here tom turkey to the meat locker."

Ollie led the way, followed by Tensleep Tom, who, needless to say, had no fear of meeting the other galoot, but who, understandably, did not like the pistol barrel in his ribs, and thus marched awkwardly.

When Ollie Oddjob unlocked the door to the basement, he was knocked backwards by a rush of simian bodies, the one baboon having presumably liberated his fellows; now all of them were eager to come upstairs to see how the other half lived. This unexpected barrage bowled over the fry cook and caused Tensleep Tom and Laramie Larry to flatten themselves against the wall. As the baboons rushed by, the front door was flung open by Cheyenne Charlie, who jumped back and let the animals loose.

In a matter of moments, the sheriff had Ollie Oddjob, Laramie Larry, and Cheyenne Charlie handcuffed and lined up against the patrol car, on charges of rustling and possession of stolen property. The baboons were bounding across the prairie. Meanwhile Wyoma and Wynema, alert to the two fugitives who had left at mention of the law, now brought them forward, each in a hammerlock. Penny walked behind them, coiling their lassos.

"We don't have much time," said Tensleep Tom, who, having removed his mustachios, began to resume the demeanor of the man bedecked in black. "You'll make it a lot easier on yourself," he said to Ollie Oddjob, "if you tell us where the boss went."

"Don't matter to me," replied the cook.

"You didn't actually do any rustling," said the sheriff.

"No."

"But you could be implicated."

"Don't matter."

"Or you could tell us where the boss went."

"Don't matter." The fry cook spit on the ground, and then he nodded in the direction of the ramshackle barn. "He went to the old barn to meet the doctor."

"The doctor with the German name?" queried the sheriff, who had apparently had some details sketched in rather quickly.

"Yeah, Hackmesser."

"How was the doctor getting here?" interrogated the sheriff.

"By helicopter."

The Ramrod Rider, as much himself as anybody now, unhitched his horse and sprang to the saddle. "We've got no time to lose," he said in his own voice.

"Don't worry," said the sheriff. "When you get there, you ought to find some help. I have a deputy coming down from Dry Creek on horseback."

A Voice from the Past, A Glance at the Future

As the Ramrod Rider drew near the ramshackle barn, he saw that activity had come to a halt there. A helicopter sat with blades immobile, and Daniel Durant's powder-blue pickup stood quiet and still with the doors open. Against the outer wall of the barn stood six men, all under the watchful eye of a deputy sheriff, who stood with his hand on a holstered pistol.

Drawing even closer, the rider identified the four hired men who had left with Daniel Durant, the malignant Doctor

Hackmesser in his homburg and Vandyke, and a sixth man who, by virtue of his headgear, figured most reasonably as the helicopter pilot. The big fish, Daniel Durant, seemed to have slipped through the net.

The rider drew rein, tipping his hat to the deputy. "Good work, deputy. Looks like you've got your hands full."

"Things happened pretty fast. I got here just as the helicopter was touching down and the pickup was pulling up. I got these two hombres," he said, waving at the doctor and the pilot, "under cover fast, and I got these four," waving at Durant's specimens, "under cover before they even got out of the pickup box."

"How about the kingpin?" inquired the rider.

"He got away. While these yahoos were climbing out of the pickup, that slick jasper took my horse."

"I'll go after him," declared the rider, reining his eager horse around.

"You be careful," said the deputy. "He looks like a dangerous one, and he's got my saddle gun."

"Will do," said the rider, touching his spurs to the sorrel horse and leaving the deputy in a cloud of dust.

The rider let the horse out, allowing it to lope at a rate that covered ground well but would not fag the horse quickly. In a short while, the pair crossed the downed fence, as yet unrepaired, of course, and followed the retreating hoofprints in the direction of Dry Creek.

When the barn at Dry Creek came into view, so did a horse and rider at some distance beyond it. In size and fugitive aspect, the rider seemed most certainly to be Daniel Durant, with the exceptional detail that he had acquired, perhaps from his pickup cab, a hat, the better to protect his moulting head from the prairie sun. Moreover it was a black hat, not unlike the hat that the Ramrod Rider himself was wont to wear.

The black hat tripped a switch in the rider's mind. He was reminded of a poem, bold words that came to him now in the eidetic image of a yellowed sheet of thick paper, with verses inscribed in a flowing hand:

Durango Dan

a fragment
by Tex Barnes

Durango Dan is a dangerous man, with a hog-leg on
    his hip,
A dark black hat with a crown that's flat, and a sneer
    upon his lip.
At midnight bold from the outside cold he walks
    through the barroom door,
The air's a-tingle with his spurs a-jingle across the
    sawdust floor.

He lights a cigar at the end of the bar, calls for a bottle
    of rye,
He downs his drink with a wince and a wink, then
    breathes a quiet sigh.
With a weathered and tanned but steady left hand he

pours from the bottle again,
And with an icy stare that would cow a bear, he says to
the gathered men:

The man I seek has a scar on his cheek and a flicker in
his eye.
He rides alone on a steeldust roan and he wants to see
me die.
When he comes to town to hunt me down, tell him I'm
glad he's here,
'Cause it's open season and I've got no reason to know
the name of fear.

That was it; the rider remembered it clearly. It was a single loose sheet of paper he had found in the memoirs of the
original Ramrod Rider, pages written in a ruder hand and
blunter style than the poem's. These memoirs had been in the
saddlebags entrusted to the Ramrod Rider at the beginning of
his present career. He had not as yet had the leisure to peruse
the narrative, and now he resolved more firmly than ever to do
so at the earliest possibility.

Meanwhile, the chase was on in earnest. Durant, for a man
of his large size, rode with surprising agility and dexterous
horsemanship, riding light in the stirrups and thus facilitating
the labor of the deputy's horse. Meanwhile, the sorrel horse, a
true cow pony, intuited the object of the chase, and directed
his pace with zeal. The Ramrod Rider felt the bond, the
kinship, of man and beast working together with purpose.
Entranced by the steady rhythm of the fleeting horse, the

drumming of hooves on the solid prairie, and the mingled smell of sagebrush, grass, and dirt, the rider thrilled again to the sensation of being transported, taken back to the cave and beyond, to become one of one, not third of three, the timeless and prevailing Ramrod Rider.

The black hat bobbed up and over a swell in the prairie ocean. Thought the Ramrod Rider, he will not disappear like the antelope did. The chase had a familiar sense to it, not as if it had all happened before, but as if it *were* happening before. The drumming of the hoofbeats brought a rush to the rider's veins. This was life as he had always known it, life full to the brim with unquestioned danger and unswerving purpose.

The black hat came into view again, the man still riding steadily, now due west. West lay the Laramie Range and Sybille Canyon, rugged counterparts to the grassy plain now fleeting beneath the hooves of the Ramrod Rider's steed.

As mile after mile flowed beneath and behind, the Ramrod Rider developed a sense of mild wonder. They had not come to a fence or a road. He had not seen a windmill. He had not seen tumbleweeds or tire tracks since leaving Dry Creek.

Then he saw ancient, shaggy forms. At first he thought they might be cattle, dark looming bovine beasts on the distant plain as Daniel Durant veered to the north of them. Drawing closer, the Ramrod Rider saw them for what they were: buffalo. Now he knew beyond all doubt that the chase was reduced to its most elemental terms. He was a lone rider, unarmed, pursuing a dangerous lone rider, in wild and open country.

Ahead lay the lower reaches of the Laramie Range; to the south lay Sybille Canyon, and to the north, Laramie Peak. The sun was beginning to slip in the western sky, and the Ramrod Rider, no new hand to old trails, realized that nightfall came quickly in and about the mountains. If he did not catch his man soon, it was beginning to become apparent, the devious Daniel Durant might make away in the oncoming night, which was likely again to be without much moonlight.

The black hat veered to the left, into the direction of the Sybille, country that looked to be rocky and rugged. Such country made for slow travel and poor trailing, even in good daylight. It was also auspicious for a man with a Winchester, who might like to rimrock his pursuer. These were the thoughts of the Ramrod Rider as he nudged his horse to move faster. Now, thought the rider, it was either make a cap or spoil a coonskin.

He began to gain perceptibly on Durant as the latter reached the rocky country. Shadows were beginning to lengthen on the shady side of the mountain, so that the dark hat became less easy to follow.

The first bullet went *spang!* on a rock at trailside, and then it was followed by the booming report of the rifle, crashing in the thin cooling air. Placing the shot, the Ramrod Rider saw movement, as the outlaw took to the trail again.

"Just tryin' to scare us off," he said to the horse.

The second shot, moments later, creased a furrow in the crown of his hat, a feature that might add character to later appearances of Tensleep Tom, but that rang a bell of caution with the present inhabitant. Pitching from the saddle, he rolled in the dirt, pulling the horse by the reins. The third shot, singing through empty air, he imagined to be sent as an encouragement to stay where he was. As he debated inwardly with himself, the Ramrod Rider saw the silhouette of horse and rider as they angled away as on a plateau.

"One more push," he said to the horse as he vaulted into the saddle. The horse, sweaty but obedient, picked his way up the trail.

Immediately prior to cresting the slope, the rider had a thought: before long it would be too dark to shoot, as well as too dark to trail. If he saw nothing from the top of this rise, he would make camp and see what the morning brought.

This might have been the final thought of the Ramrod Rider, for, as he crested upon the plateau, he saw, at a distance of less than a hundred yards, a man on a horse, wearing a black hat and aiming a rifle. But with the lightning-quick reflexes of a man whose sense of danger never slept, he kicked the sorrel in one direction and bailed off in the other. The bullet whistled between horse and rider.

As the Ramrod Rider rolled in the flinty soil and sparse grass, he saw the other man's horse begin to buck and pitch. The man was a rider. Reining the horse and keeping his balance, Durant managed to slip the Winchester back into its scabbard. All the while, he did not lose the black hat. Intent as he was on securing the rifle in its boot, however, he must not have seen that the horse had brought them near a drop-off. Had he seen, he would undoubtedly have stepped off the horse as calmly as a bronc rider asking for a re-ride. As the horse spun and bucked, its rear hooves slipped over the edge;

continuing its rhythm, the horse pitched backward, so that the Ramrod Rider had a disappearing view of the horse's belly, its nostrils flared in a mixture of fury and fear, and beyond that, the startled face of a man in a black hat.

There followed an eerie scream, a sound not recognizable to the Ramrod Rider as coming from either man or beast. It was a scream of agony and terror, and then there was no sound.

The rider crept to the canyon rim and peered over. The descent was steep and shaly, and already the dusk was so thick he could make out nothing more certain than a sprawled and motionless horse. He resolved to make camp and upon the morning make a closer examination. Picketing his horse, he had a small meal of water, jerky, and hardtack—frugal fare for a hard man in hard country. Then, with the steamy saddle blanket as his only cover in the chilling mountain air, and cautiously denying himself the comfort of a fire, he drifted to light sleep.

* * * * *

In the morning, having made his perilous descent, he found the lifeless horse and the damaged saddle. Although the bulk of the horse had covered the scabbard and made removal of the Winchester well-nigh impossible, the carbine was gone, as was Daniel Durant. Had the nimble outlaw sprung free from the wreckage, effecting extrication of the Winchester as he did so? To this question the Ramrod Rider had no empirical answer, for he found no prints or other marks that might tell of

Durant's fate. It was as if the man in the black hat, last seen in mid-air, had vanished from that point.

* * * * *

Back at the ranch some hours later, still in the garb of Tensleep Tom and visibly weathered from the trail, the Ramrod Rider gave a modest narrative of his adventure to Penny and Puncher, the latter having relinquished his jail cell to the estimable tenant in the homburg hat. Puncher, glancing in the direction of the secretive mountains, said, "He might be up there still, in one piece, or he might be workin' his way through a buzzard's gizzard."

"I have a hunch," offered the Ramrod Rider, "that he might turn up somewhere again."

"It's a cinch he won't come back to the Leanin' Wye," declared Puncher. "If he does, it's a short trip to the hoosegow for him." He took a drink of lemonade and smacked his lips in satisfaction.

"Well," said the Ramrod Rider, "I probably ought to be gettin' back to my regular duds."

Stepping outside the ranch house, he saw the familiar red Dodge pickup stopping in the driveway, bearing as its cargo the vivacious Wyoma and Wynema. One of them was driving. As he walked down the plank steps, the twin cowgirls bounced out of the pickup and exclaimed together, "It's Tensleep Tom!" Then, pressing up against him like the double D's in Dodge, they kissed him on the face.

"Waal," he said, blushing beneath the double implants of lipstick but endeavoring to speak in the character of his alter ego, "yer orter give a man fair warnin'!"

At this the girls each kissed him again and bounded, giggling, into the house.

In a thrice he was again the Ramrod Rider, bedecked in black and himself to the last detail. Having fulfilled his mission, he was, as he expressed to the quartet on the porch, "ready to see some new country."

"Puss and I just can't tell you how much we appreciate it," said Puncher, clearly moved beyond the capacity of self-expression.

The Ramrod Rider, himself a man of few words, tipped his hat brim and said, "My pleasure."

Then he was gone in a small cloud of dust—just a small cloud, for as he looked in his rear view mirror, he was quite sure he saw, from two of the people on the porch, a double wink intended for the Ramrod Rider.

Rocky Mountain Rendezvous

Introducing the White Arrow and an Old Scout

Let us open our story in the poetic spirit:

'Twas in the autumn of the year
When yellow leaves were falling,
When moonlight played on virgin snow
And coyotes were a-calling.

It was also that time of year when hunters took to the high country, to search the timber and meadows for Rocky Mountain elk. On a sunny day in October—the fourteenth, to be exact—throngs of hunters drove westward out of Laramie, Wyoming, in pickups, sport utility vehicles, and motor homes. Alone in this caravan, seeming to take part in the pageantry, a black pickup wended its way. Inside the cab, the early afternoon sun came through the windshield and shone upon the features of the man, bedecked in black, who called himself the Ramrod Rider.

In this part of the Rocky Mountains (which the reader can find on a map and thus verify the truthfulness of this narrative), elk season was scheduled to open on October 15. Thus the vehicles would be brimful of hunting necessities: orange apparel, ammunition, Vienna sausages, packaged pastries, sundry foodstuffs, propane, white gas, beer, and antacid.

While the man in black had his own meager and comparative-
ly Spartan provisions, with not a can of Vienna sausages or
Dinty Moore beef stew in his outfit, it nevertheless behooved
him to have on display some of the accoutrements and outer
emblems of the nimrod. Above and behind the bench seat in
the pickup cab, a gun rack cradled a lever-action Winchester;
on the dashboard rode a box of .30-30 shells and a spool of
orange surveyor's ribbon. The Ramrod Rider was on a hunting
expedition, but unlike the other hunters in the serpentine
convoy, he had as his quarry a human.

Hold, gentle reader, and do not think for a moment that
the dedicated rider of the mountains and plains would consider
pointing Monsieur Winchester at a fellow human. Nay, the
rifle and the cartridges and the orange ribbon all played but a
role in the promenade. In the successive guises of elk hunter
and forest ranger, the Ramrod Rider hoped to find his way to
the mountain lair of a fugitive from justice. For it had come to
his attention that somewhere in the frigid vastness of the
Snowy Range (for such was the name of this part of the Rocky
Mountains), keeping himself inconspicuous and no doubt
devising new evil, lurked Daniel Durant.

Some readers may recall this personage, who made his
exit from the pages of history (and from the eye of man) on
the rim of the Sybille Canyon. It is doubtful that he floated in
air for the interval, but one way or the other, he had reportedly
landed nearly a hundred miles to the southwest, some months
later in the same year. Now it was the Ramrod Rider's mission
to locate him, to make sure of his man, and to help draw the
net of justice around him.

To that end, he had arranged to leave his pickup at a ranger station, where he would be fitted out with a saddle horse and appurtenant gear. On horseback he could cross country that was closed to motor vehicles; also, he could disassociate himself from the black pickup and merge into his two roles of hunter and ranger.

By late afternoon, the Ramrod Rider arrived at the ranger station. There he acquired a horse and a double-rigged saddle, suitable for mountain riding, plus a bridle, halter, and picket rope. He saddled the horse, tied on his minimal camp kit and comestibles, and in a scabbard secured the ubiquitous Winchester.

Having been informed of a large parcel of fenced private land, the rider kept to the main road for a few miles as he headed from a sagebrush flat into the towering mountains. Then he turned off of the main road, let the dark horse pick its way down a slope to a creek bottom, crossed the creek, and followed it upstream into the heart of the country. For now he was in the Medicine Bow National Forest, where shaggy timber brought early, cold shadows.

The country was sublime in its autumnal splendor. The aspens, which grew in patches and groves amidst the dark timber, had turned yellow and would soon be bare. A recent snowfall had left about six inches of snow in all but the sunniest places, and many of the lofty evergreens still had snow on the branches. The air was clean and pure, and the early evening chill gave a sharp edge to the rider's senses. Thus alert to his new surroundings, he rode on in quietness, the horse's hooves falling on a carpet of snow.

This country was penetrated by numerous dirt roads, which generally followed streams, canyons, and passes. Many such roads were well travelled, especially during hunting season; but in between the roads, where the huge mountains rose to meet the endless sky, lay large tracts of land that felt no harsher touch than that of an animal hoof or hiking boot. Having studied a map at the ranger station, the Ramrod Rider chose to cross such an area.

Under other circumstances he would pitch his camp in a covert place, far from the glint of camper trailers and the snarl of chain saws, but during hunting season, one was better advised to camp in plain view—the better to keep the tent from being perforated with large-caliber bullet holes, and the better to safeguard the horse's longevity into the next week. Therefore the Ramrod Rider planned to set his camp not far from a road, thus resembling an elk hunter in manner and prudence.

Happy was he, this newly arrived nimrod on the eve of elk season, to find a grassy sward with a creek tumbling by, and a road perhaps a hundred yards distant. It was the work of a few moments, then, to strip the horse and picket it, set up the pup tent, tie orange ribbons on the guy ropes, and store his gear. Then he gathered firewood, and in a circular campfire pit he found close by, he built a fire on top of the last campers' crushed and melted beer cans.

Shadows grew quickly as the sun slipped behind the peaks to the west. The droning of a distant chain saw finally died, so that all that could be heard was the wind in the pines and an occasional pickup rattling in to the back country. Then night came on completely, a luminous night, for the beams of a three-quarter moon flooded down upon the snow. The magic of a high-country night became complete when a coyote sent its wail into the mountain air. The Ramrod Rider, no stranger to such nights, rolled out his bed and slept the sleep of the untroubled.

* * * * *

Came the dawn, and with it the sounds of motor vehicles, among them the four-wheeled motorcycle, or four-wheeler, now much favored by sportsmen. The Ramrod Rider emerged from his pup tent, still in the garb of the dark rider, but with the addition of a netted blaze orange vest, in compliance with Wyoming hunting regulations. His plan was to make one reconnaissance thus attired and then to sally forth, somewhat later, in a new guise.

The morning sun shed warmth upon the land as the Ramrod Rider rode out upon the morning and followed a dirt road north. As it was the opening morning of the season, he heard rifle shots off in the distance, and before long he met his first successful hunters—two grinning fat men, swathed in orange, rumbling along in an economy-size pickup with Wisconsin license plates. The four dark legs of an elk protruded over the passenger's side of the pickup box. As the vehicle rolled past him, the rider on horseback looked down and saw the scarcely-antlered head wedged against the tailgate.

"Spike," he said, as he lowered his hand from waving at the men in the machine.

Onward he rode, noting the locations and kinds of camps along the road. This far into the mountains he did not see motor homes, but he did see a wide variety of camper trailers, pickup campers, and tents. Most of the camps lay close to the road, partly for reasons of convenience and partly because of the new White Arrow code, which was in effect along this thoroughfare. The new code or regulation restricted motor vehicle traffic from venturing more than one hundred yards off the main road in posted areas—a restriction that would certainly disappoint the operators of four wheelers. These vehicles lived up to their commercial name of All-Terrain Vehicles. Where once a pair of hunters might have labored half a day or more to drag an animal, a single man could now, with the help of a chain saw, clear a path and drag an animal from the deep reaches of the forest—much to the envy of his fellow hunters, who might stand slack-jawed with beer cans halfway to their mouths as the prideful hunter came bouncing into camp with a carcass in tow.

The Ramrod Rider respected the right of his fellow adventurers to have a quality experience in the outdoors, but in those places where restrictions were in effect, he would fain see the rules followed. He had been briefed on the White Arrow code at the ranger station and had volunteered to help uphold it, thus to help protect the environment of the bounteous West from the onslaught of petroleum, steel, and rubber.

By mid-morning, after he had ridden several miles from his own camp, he observed that hunters were returning from the morning hunt. As the snow was now beginning to melt and form rivulets in the road, passing vehicles made a subdued slushing sound. The four-wheelers, with their waffle-grid tires, also threw up a fine brown spray in their passage—of which some of the precipitation settled upon the drivers and their rifles. Nearly every hunter waved, and those on four-wheelers did also, flashing the clean palm of a hand or the white gleam of a smile from beneath the mantle of mud.

At length the Ramrod Rider decided he would turn back, having scouted out a long stretch of the road and having seen excellent compliance with the White Arrow code. Just as he was on the verge of turning around, his attention was drawn to a campsite off the road to his right and up on a knoll. A pickup not unlike his own sat in the forefront of the site, with a bolt-action rifle hanging scope downward in the gun rack. Feeling an inexplicable kinship with the denizen of the camp, he was moved to make his acquaintance.

Thus he turned off the roadside and headed the dark horse toward the camp. As the Ramrod Rider approached the campsite, he saw a person sitting on a camp chair in front of a large canvas wall tent. This person was somewhere in middle age, with a dark beard giving way to grey. The man wore an orange hunting cap, a wool hunting jacket of austere olive drab, and a pair of trousers of faded blue denim. The man in the chair smiled at the approach of the rider.

"Hello the camp," said the rider as he drew near.

"Hello to the dark stranger," returned the other man. "They call me the Old Scout, and this is my tent and camp. Pile off your horse for a minute or two."

At this juncture the Ramrod Rider observed that the man had a notebook and pen resting atop a knapsack on the ground beside the chair. In his lap he had a paper napkin, with a granola bar holding it down, and on his left knee he had an as yet unravished orange. "I hope I'm not disturbing your snack," said the rider as he dismounted.

"Not at all," said the Old Scout. "Happy to have company. And since I've told you who I am, tell me, stranger, who you are, so that I may know you."

The Ramrod Rider noticed that despite the greying beard, the man had sparkling green eyes that expressed a youthful spirit matching his own. He returned the man's smile, and then, much to his own surprise, he felt a spirit move within himself and, as if guided by a power that brings poetic light to dark places, he broke into spontaneous musical recitation.

Song of the Ramrod Rider

From California to Wyoming
    And on down to Mexico,
I campaign for truth and justice
    In the places where I go.

I'm an orphan without memory
    Of a mother or a dad—
And I truly can't remember
    Any early life I had.

But a few years back it happened
    As the hand of Destiny
Took the blank slate of my memory

And re-wrote a role for me.

"You can be the Ramrod Rider,"
    Said the man who took me in,
"For as you can see, I'm dyin',
    And I've got no kith or kin—

"And I've got but few possessions,
    Just this little leather pack,
Which contains the early memoirs
    Of the man bedecked in black.

"Just this bag, a few provisions,
    And my saddlebags, of course,
Plus my six-guns and my saddle,
    And my faithful, trusty horse.

"Like the man who went before me,
    I will pass it on to you,
With the hope that truth and justice
    Will inspire all you do."

And with that my mentor faded
    Like the sunset in the west,
And I saw his eyelids flutter
    As I pledged to do my best.

Then alone I took possession
    Of the little leather pack,

And the guns and horse and saddle
    Of the man bedecked in black.

Now throughout the West I wander,
    Like the two that went before,
In defense of the downtrodden,
    The beleaguered and the poor.

I call myself the Ramrod Rider,
    I'm the third such man of three—
If you believe in truth and justice,
    Then you've got a friend in me.

"Well, mighty fine," said the Old Scout, who had seemed on the verge of driving his right thumbnail into the rind of the orange but now paused on the brink of that exertion. "Usually, if I drop into poetry, I do it in heroic couplets, with maybe an alexandrine tossed in to flavor the stew, but I'll be happy to try singin' a rejoinder in your own meter." With that, he launched into the following:

Song of the Old Scout

I was born in California,
    What they call the Golden State,
Down in Santa Barbara County
    In the year of '48.

Out-of-staters by the thousands
    Proved to be too much for me,
So I came to wide Wyoming
    Where a young man could be free.

I have seen a thousand wonders
    In our many-splendored state
And been dealt a hundred heartaches
    By the vagaries of Fate.

For in quest of love long-lasting,
    I have struggled all the way,
And though women are well-meaning,
    They have turned my whiskers grey.

I have loved Wyoming's rivers,
    And her sagebrush plains and creeks,
And I've oft beheld the mountains
    With their distant, stirring peaks.

And I love my fellow creatures
    From the elk down to the mole;
I've embraced the furry bunnies
    And I believe I share their soul—

For there's one great soul that binds us
    From the moment of our birth;
It's the soul that brings together
    All the living things on earth.

And this great transcendent Spirit
 Doesn't stop with flesh and blood,
But includes each tree and sagebrush,
 Every flower, leaf, and bud.

I'm at peace with my surroundings
 In the bosom of the West,
But despite my bond with Nature,
 There's a turmoil in my breast.

For the women I have courted
 Have all left me soon or late,
So I've come to these high mountains
 To reflect and meditate.

Day by day I write my memoirs,
 And I hope before I die
I will meet yet one more woman
 And give love another try.

The Ramrod Rider nodded in comprehension, and as he did so, the Old Scout said, "I could have gone on quite a bit longer about my Byronic sorrows, but I wanted to keep to the same number of stanzas." Then he added, looking at the notebook at his side, "Of course, my main interest right now is in writing my memoirs, where I am developing the theme at satisfactory length."

"Memoirs?" said the rider.

"Yes," responded the Old Scout. "Writing down the events of one's life. Getting one's life story on paper."

"Oh, yes," said the Ramrod Rider. In his memory, a form moved as if beneath a blanket of leaves.

"You look lost in thought," said the Old Scout.

"Huh?" said the rider, shaking his head. "Oh, yes. Memoirs. Uh-huh. I was just rememberin' that an—uh—ancestor of mine had left behind some memoirs, and every now and then I remember 'em, but I've never gotten around to readin' the actual pages. But I've got 'em."

"Is that so?" said the Old Scout, setting his hat back about an inch without bringing a hairline into view. "That must be what you referred to in your song. Those memoirs might be interesting."

"And as far as I know," said the rider, "no one outside the family has read 'em."

"Well," said the Old Scout, "I hope you take good care of them." The green eyes sparkled. "That's how we speak across time," he said. "With the recorded word. Nowadays, people have tape recorders and video cameras and who knows what-all. But for centuries, it's been the written word." He glanced at the notebook. "My own memoirs, modest though they be, will have the power to speak to generations hence, long after any beneficiaries of mine have ceased to reap the tangential benefits of my passing."

The rider gave him a questioning look.

"Money. After they've spent any money I leave, and after they've sold my guns and tents and spent that, too."

"Oh," said the rider. Then glancing at the rifle in the pickup cab, he said, "You do hunt. You're not just here to work on your memoirs."

"Certainly," replied the Old Scout. "Self-professed bunny-hugger that I am, I do shed the blood of the beast. *Il faut manger.*"

"Meanin'?" queried the rider.

"It is necessary to eat." The Old Scout smiled, then continued by way of explanation. "Life must feed on other life. It's part of the big plan." The Old Scout glanced again at the notebook. "But while I'm here, I also jot down a sentence or two from time to time." He smiled and looked back at his youthful visitor. "Can I offer you something to eat or drink?"

"No, thanks," replied the rider. "I'm about to head back to my own camp."

"Well, good luck," said the Old Scout. "I hope you find an elk."

"The same to you," said the Ramrod Rider, who turned the horse around and mounted it. A few yards out, he turned around and saw the Old Scout taking a bite on the granola bar as he moved pen across paper, scratching words that might be interesting to someone, generations hence.

A Gleam of Silver

The snow continued to melt, and the roads became muddier. Passing pickups were now muddy up to the rear-view mirrors, and four-wheelers looked like peanut clusters that had been dipped in chocolate. When possible, the Ramrod Rider kept the horse a few yards from the road, but in some places, because of the steepness of the roadside or the closeness of the timber, he was obliged to take to the road.

At one point on his return, as he was following a game and cattle trail about fifteen yards to the left of the road, he saw an unassuming camp that lay farther back among the pines. With a quick estimate, the Ramrod Rider satisfied himself that the camp was well within the boundaries of the White Arrow. The camp consisted mainly of an old, silver-colored camp trailer, now gleaming in the morning sunlight, and an old Dodge pickup of a faded aqua complexion. The pickup was parked perpendicular to the trailer, nose to nose, with the tail end of the pickup facing the road. The Ramrod Rider observed the dented rear fender, the dual wheels, the rusty tailgate . . . and then a movement caught his eye.

The door of the trailer had opened, and a man was stepping outside. He was dressed in military camouflage and was holding a white enamel basin in front of him. With a quick motion he pitched the steaming contents of the basin into the snow, shook the basin, and looked around. The man had a balding blond head and a light-colored beard shot with silver; but despite the beard, there was no mistaking his identity. It was Daniel Durant.

If the man took any notice of a passing horse and rider, he gave no indication. He lowered the basin with his right hand and turned back toward the trailer. Stepping up on a wooden crate that was placed before the entry, he reached with his left hand for the door, which he pulled behind him as he disappeared into the silver-colored shell.

The Ramrod Rider, whose pulse had quickened at the sight of his nemesis, now regained his calm composure. Here was the man he sought! Now he need only observe him more closely to be sure of the man's circumstances, and then summon the myrmidons of justice. For closer observation he decided to wait until dark, which came early at this time of year in the mountains.

To help pass the time agreeably, the Ramrod Rider turned away from the main thoroughfare and followed a trail that led uphill through a broad, open drainage between two timbered ridges. At this time of day he would probably not be interfering with someone else's hunt, and if he kept to the open, he and the horse would be visible and therefore less likely to draw fire.

He rode for about two miles, enjoying the sun and the breeze and the far-reaching blue sky. Presently he saw two hunters coming down the slope toward him on foot, so he dismounted, that he might not be looking down on them when they met—a point of etiquette observed by the more courteous of elk hunters on horseback.

The pedestrian hunter in front was a middle-aged man of average height, tending toward heaviness and a drooping girth. He wore field boots, baggy khaki pants, a quilted winter parka with a loose vest of hunter orange, and a felt hat. He had a brown beard, speckled with white, and a pair of brown-rimmed glasses. Slung over his shoulder was a rifle, and on his right hip hung a large sheath knife with a knotted leather thong hanging from it.

His young companion, who was dragging his feet a few steps behind, came clomping up with his mouth agape. He, too, had an orange vest and winter coat, but not neatly fastened like the older man's. He also had a rifle slung on his shoulder, and he wore the additional adornment of a bandoleer, which held about thirty cartridges and from which dangled a hunting knife in its sheath. The young man wore no headgear, so that his uncombed hair was prominently on display.

The older man spoke, and he did so with all the natural charm of a gentleman emigrant from West Virginia. "Where's all the big ones?" he asked.

The Ramrod Rider merely waggled his eyebrows and smiled.

"There's game here," said the older man, who now brought a half-smoked cigar into view and took a puff off of the soggy end. "But when the season's here—why, hush, they're out of sight. Ah come up here in Joo-lye, and ah saw two mule deer bucks that a man would lose sleep over. The big one would go two hunnerd in Boone and Crockett."

The Ramrod Rider nodded.

"But ah come back in deer season, and they're nowhere to be found. Then rat up on that ridge—" he pointed backwards with his right thumb— "ah saw a fahve-point bull elk. That was two weeks ago. Now we sat there for three hours this morning, and all we saw was other hunters."

"And a kah-yo-tee," added the young man.

"That, too," said the senior hunter. Then he peered at the Ramrod Rider and delivered the most commonly posed query in elk country. "Seen anything?"

The Ramrod Rider shook his head in the negative.

The older man lifted his head with an air of superior wisdom. "We've just got to keep lookin', that's wot." He hitched the sling of the rifle with his thumb, and with a jerk of his head he signalled to his younger companion. Turning back around to face the man in black, he said, "Good luck to ya," and tipped his hat, as perhaps he had learned to do in his southern homeland.

At the top of the slope, the Ramrod Rider dismounted and looked over the country. At his feet he saw where the two hunters had spent the morning. In addition to a cigar butt, he saw two soft drink cans, two candy bar wrappers, an empty smokeless tobacco can with its lid nearby, and a plastic-and-cardboard package that had once held two size-A batteries. The Ramrod Rider thought of the Old Scout and how he would probably frown on such promiscuous littering. Withdrawing a small plastic bag from his saddlebag, the Ramrod Rider picked up the debris and stowed it in the plastic bag, which he in turn secured once again in his saddlebag.

He shook his head. He did not have time (nor the inclination) to go around and pick up after everyone, but when the evidence of such heedless behavior stood squarely in his way, he could stoop for a moment and do a good deed in service to the environment.

Returning to the uplifting experience of surveying the majestic country, the Ramrod Rider thought again of the Old

Scout, who, despite the sorrows of romantic disappointments, could stand on a promontory such as this and feel a oneness with all of Nature. Then the Ramrod Rider gazed at the soft earth, dampened by the melting snow and roughed up by the heels of the two hunters who had sat there. Perhaps they, too, had enjoyed nature, and it was likely that they had left their trash out of ignorance rather than malice.

The Ramrod Rider looked back in the direction whence he had come. Yes, he thought, there were others more blameworthy—men who deliberated and schemed, men who recked not the value of life or of the gifts of Nature.

Thus sobered by reflection upon the man whose presence had brought him to this panoramic country, the Ramrod Rider mounted the dark horse and rode back downhill toward his camp.

With his horse on picket, the Ramrod Rider sat at the entrance to his pup tent and ate a modest repast of crackers and cheese. He knew that in the other camps, hunters were now taking their noonday rest, enjoying camaraderie and exchanging knowledge, sharing the small cans of Vienna sausage, perhaps eating sardines and potato chips, and quaffing cool beverages. Those were the pleasures of men who came for sport and recreation. For the lone rider, the pursuit of truth and justice knew no vacation.

Although he had no true leisure, he was obliged to loiter away the afternoon until, under cover of darkening night, he might make his reconnaissance.

As the shadows lengthened and then merged with the dusk, the rider bestirred himself and saddled the dark horse.

Then he took to the trail, having first put on a warm winter coat, for the temperature was dropping quickly.

He tied the horse to a small aspen tree about a quarter mile from the silver trailer, then proceeded on foot over the soft ground. Just as he reached his destination, a vehicle turned off the main road and drove toward the trailer. The Ramrod Rider sank back into the shadows and watched the vehicle approach.

Presently it came to a stop, and he saw the vehicle clearly—a shiny, new sport utility vehicle, dark blue and green in the light that poured out of the trailer window. It had three different kinds of antennae, the likes of which the Ramrod Rider had seen on limousines and other luxurious touring cars. The front passenger door opened, and a light came on to reveal a plush interior and a uniformed driver. The passenger, a small man in a suit and a homburg hat, stepped out of the vehicle and closed the door, leaving the chauffeur in relative darkness. Then he went to the trailer and rapped on the metal siding.

The door opened, and Durant's voice came out. "Well, hello, Dr. Kaufenkopf. I see you found your way."

"Yes," said the little man. "Your directions are quite precise."

"Please come in."

"Thank you."

The Ramrod Rider took this occasion to move around to the back side of the trailer, where he found a window which was cranked open about an inch—presumably for ventilation. Crouching beside the window, he tuned his eyes and ears to the scene within.

The visitor was taking off his coat, which was a fur-lined garment made of herringbone wool. Durant took the coat and then the man's hat and put them in a small closet.

"A drink, perhaps?" offered the host.

"Very well," said the doctor, who was now quite visible. He had a trim grey beard, a bald head, and round, wire-rimmed glasses.

"A glass of Gamay Beaujolais—no," said Durant, interrupting himself. "I think I should offer you a taste of Johannisberg Riesling."

The visitor smiled. "Very good."

The host forthwith brought out a bottle and went about extracting the cork, during which activity the Ramrod Rider observed the furnishings of the trailer.

The interior was quite commodious, and far more elegant than the exterior would lead one to expect. The very front of the trailer contained the kitchen area, complete with a microwave oven and a small television set, a stove and refrigerator, and a dinette booth with two bench seats. The living room, paneled and carpeted, had a sofa and a computer station, the latter situated on a handsome piece of cabinetry. A hallway from the living room apparently led to one or more bedrooms.

The lord of the manor held two glasses of white wine and extended one to his guest. Then holding his own glass up and out to meet the other man hob and nob, he said, "To a successful venture."

The doctor squinted as he smiled, and raising his glass so that it was reflected in his wire-rimmed spectacles, he said, "Let us hope so."

Durant took a sip and said, "You come highly recommended from your colleague, Doctor Hackmesser."

"A good man," said the doctor. "And a true scientist. I was quite sorry to learn he was being . . . detained."

"We've got a couple of good Denver lawyers working on it," said Durant. "He should be free by the end of the year."

"Let us hope so," said the little man, delivering the phrase as if it were an automatic item in his repertoire.

"Meanwhile, let us move forward."

"Very well."

"Time may be of the essence," said Durant. "There is a cold air mass moving in, and either tomorrow night or the next night, the temperature should plummet—that is, it should drop very quickly."

"Yass."

"And when it drops that quickly, with the attendant changes in atmospheric pressure and electrical resistance, we will have optimum conditions that cannot be simulated in a laboratory."

"You mean, of course, for the cryonic preservation of heads."

"Exactly."

"And you have the two—specimens?"

Durant smiled in the manner of a proud owner. "They should be back any minute. I sent them out hunting."

"I see. It was quite generous of you to offer me two heads, since I could not have hoped for more than one for my initial experiment."

Durant's ruddy cheeks gleamed, and his blue eyes sparkled. "Like the taxidermist says, two heads are better than one."

"Ha, ha, ha!" cried the doctor, shaking with laughter. "That is very funny!"

Durant, visibly pleased with his own wit, continued. "You've heard of the mastodons that were frozen instantly with the vegetation still in their mouths?"

"Ah, yes. Incredible! Beautiful."

"Well, that's how we'll have these two. But instead of grass in their mouths, they'll have Copenhagen."

The doctor looked puzzled. "Denmark?" he queried.

"No," said Durant, quickly. "It's a type of tobacco that they chew."

The doctor seemed to take a moment to absorb the knowledge, and then he tittered with laughter. "Very good, Durant. You are quite excellent to make jokes."

Durant smiled. "One more joke before they get here."

The doctor tilted his chin upward. "Go ahead."

Durant sipped his wine. "You will see soon enough that these two brains will be very valuable, once harvested."

"I should ask why."

Durant paused. "They've never been used."

"Ha! ha! ha! ha! Durant, you are priceless!"

The gracious host smiled again. "Speaking literally, that is probably not true."

Presenting the Two Heads

There followed a long moment of relative silence in which neither the doctor nor his host spoke, but rather stood smiling, do doubt imbued with mirth, and savoring the sparkling white wine provided by the hospitable Durant.

Presently there came the sound of stamping feet, and the door of the trailer swung open abruptly, causing a vibration of the interior that the Ramrod Rider could sense from his place of observation. Then, as if to fill the momentary vacuum, into the trailer stepped two men.

Both were unmistakably returned from elk hunting, for they wore knitted orange caps and plastic orange vests, and upon their shoulders they had rifles with scopes. As further evidence of having been out tramping around on opening day, they were both encrusted with mud up to their hip pockets. They gave a curious glance toward the prim doctor, who in turn was looking them over thoroughly.

"We was wonderin' whose outfit that was," said one of the hunters, who was somewhat taller and leaner than his colleague.

"This is Dr. Kaufenkopf," said Daniel Durant.

The two hunters pulled off their knitted orange caps, in evident expression of respect. "Pleased t'meet you," they said together.

"It is my pleasure," said the doctor, enunciating each syllable.

"These are my hired men," said Durant. "This one," pointing at the taller of the two, "is Centennial Slim. And this one," pointing at the heavier specimen, "is Saratoga Sam."

The doctor nodded, and the two men grinned.

Durant cocked his head and knitted his eyebrows. "Go ahead and unload those smoke-poles, uh, boys?"

The hired men nodded, unslung their rifles, and pointing both of them in the direction of the Ramrod Rider's window, unloaded the firearms. Each man accomplished this task by opening the bolt action and then dropping the trapdoor in front of the trigger guard, which maneuver dropped a handful of shining cartridges into a waiting hand. Then each man clicked the trapdoor shut, slid the bolt into place, dumped the cartridges into his knit orange cap, and stored cap and rifle in the closet. With the hunting paraphernalia stored, they withdrew western hats from the closet and put them on. Through the whole process, the doctor watched.

"Are you cowboys?" he inquired.

"Seein' as how we're livin' in a trailer house, we come pretty close," replied Sam. "But we're general all-around hands. We can drive truck, run a backhoe—"

"—pour concrete, do roofin'," added Slim.

"Right now," said Durant, "they're camp helpers."

"Oh, I see," said the doctor, still casting an appraising look. Then, turning to the host, he said, "Very well, Mr. Durant, I must be going. I shall await your call."

"Certainly," said Durant, moving to the closet and taking out the doctor's hat and coat. "I have a phone in the pickup, so there won't be any delay."

The doctor put on his hat and coat, wished a good evening to the other three, and walked out.

When the doctor's vehicle could be heard backing away from the trailer, Sam and Slim began taking off their pants, which action showed that they were both wearing long underwear.

"What do you think you're doing?" asked their boss.

"Gettin' out of these wet Wranglers," said Sam.

"Not yet," snapped Durant.

Both men paused, crouching with their pants down at their knees, and looked up at Durant, who now had a wine glass once again in his hand.

"You've got work to do," he said.

The men straightened up, pulling the muddy trousers back up.

"What now?" asked Slim.

"You're supposed to be elk hunters. This is supposed to be a hunting camp. That means tacky. Now get outside, stretch out that blue plastic tarp, and make an awning in front of this trailer."

"Aw, c'mon," said Sam. "Can't we do it in the mornin'?"

"You fellows have to be out hunting with the crack of dawn. And I want this place to look right."

"Sheesh," interjected Slim. "I don't know why we've got to keep up this front, anyway."

"I'm not paying you to know anything," said Durant, "and it's a good thing I'm not."

"Can't we eat first?" pleaded Sam.

"You can eat afterwards," replied the boss.

"Microwave T.V. dinners again?" groused Slim.

"A balanced meal, as always."

Slim, who seemed to be mildly more recalcitrant than his partner, asked, "Why don't you come out and help us, then, and we'll get it done faster?"

"You forget," said Durant, taking a sip of wine. "I'm the camp cook."

Grumbling, the two hired men snugged up their jeans and, still wearing their coats and orange vests, went outside. Durant sat down at the computer station and brought the screen alive. Within a few minutes he was playing a game, which entailed shooting bunny rabbits as they bounded back and forth across the screen.

After about twenty minutes of jostling the trailer, during which time the Ramrod Rider felt the temperature around him drop perceptibly, Sam and Slim came clomping back into the well-lighted interior.

The master peeked out the door, then closed it and turned to his hired hands. "Looks fine," he said. "I knew I had the right men for the job." Then he went to the kitchen, took two packaged meals from the refrigerator, and put them into the microwave oven. With a few electronic beeps, he executed the chores of the camp cook.

"Gonna get cold tonight," said Sam, moving to a wall thermostat and putting his hand to it.

Suddenly a gasoline engine roared alive, not three feet from the Ramrod Rider, who was taken quite by surprise. Finally subduing his own surge of fear, he returned to the window, and above the roar of the engine he could hear indistinct shouting. Sam put his hand on the thermostat, and the generator went quiet again.

Not much later, the oven made a series of three beeps, and Durant withdrew the two meals and set them on the table in the dining nook. The two hired men, now in cowboy hats and long underwear, sat at the table. Centennial Slim reached into the refrigerator and brought out two cans of Old Milwaukee, and the evening meal was under way. Daniel Durant returned to his computer, with his wine glass refilled, and resumed shooting rabbits.

After a short while, the two men at the table finished their meal and threw the plastic refuse into a garbage sack. Saratoga Sam fished a deck of cards out from a kitchen drawer, while his partner Slim brought out two more cans of Old Milwaukee. The evening seemed to have settled into its pattern, with no audible conversation above the shuffle of cards, the blips and bleeps of the computer screen, and an occasional oath from one of the card players.

The Ramrod Rider, now having stood in the cold for nearly an hour, the last half of which had brought him no new intelligence, decided to return to his camp. As he walked away from the trailer he heard the generator kick on again. Had he not known what devious plans the man at the computer had in store for the two men playing cards in their long johns, he might have envied the comfort of the silver shell as the outdoor temperature grew colder and colder.

Ranger Redsleeves Makes an Appearance

At dawn, the Ramrod Rider peeked out through the flap of his pup tent and saw a world crusted with frost. He knew that the mud would be frozen solid, the puddles slick, until the morning sun should brighten the world and soften the soup. He huddled for a while longer in the relative warmth of his bedroll, then rummaged in his rucksack for the clothes he planned to wear on this day.

As the rays of the sun cleared the jagged ridges of the east, a man emerged from the pup tent. Not clad in black like the man who had gone into the tent, this man wore insulated hiking boots, blue jeans, and a heavy red wool hunting shirt, the latter held snug by a brown thermal hunting vest. Atop the man's head sat a single-billed deerstalker cap in a dashing hunter's plaid. The earflaps had been untied and let down, the better to protect the ears of Ranger Redsleeves.

This personage drew on a pair of fleece-lined suede leather gloves, then built up a fire and tended to the dark horse. After breakfast, the ranger checked the various pockets of his vest for compass, whistle, pen and notepad, orange ribbon, and granola bars. Then he saddled the dark horse, secured the Winchester in the scabbard, and rode out upon the morning.

Had circumstances been different, he might have ridden down to the ranger station to begin closing the net around Durant, but having observed Dr. Hackmesser's sinister colleague, Dr. Kaufenkopf, he decided it would be worth the gamble to try to catch that miscreant, also. Thus did he sally forth as Ranger Redsleeves, in hopes of gaining further information for making a timely apprehension.

It was an amiable Ranger Redsleeves, therefore, who ambled into the enemy camp on horseback. Daniel Durant was chopping wood, and evidence of his labor was already stacked beneath the blue awning—which, to do credit to the master of the castle, had quite the appearance he had called for. The door of the aqua-colored Dodge pickup was opened, and the radio was blaring; as Ranger Redsleeves drew near, he recognized that the radio was tuned to a full-time weather station. All elk hunters had to heed the weather, but this pretender no doubt had a greater interest in knowing the forecast for the overnight low temperature.

"Good morning," said the ranger, dismounting.

Durant sank the double-bit axe into an aspen log and straightened up. Except for a bit of mud bulging up around the soles of his snow boots, he was immaculate. He was wearing military camouflage as on the day previous, and to protect his head he was wearing a solid green, flat-topped army cap that would have done honor to Fidel Castro. "Good morning," he said. He moved to the pickup cab and turned off the radio, and while he did so, Ranger Redsleeves observed that the cab was equipped not only with a radio and a cellular telephone but also a miniature computer of the type used for electronic map reading. Durant closed the door of the pickup cab and returned his attention to his visitor.

"Hunting elk?" queried the ranger.

"This is an elk hunting camp," replied the camp tender, "but I'm not hunting."

"Oh, I see."

Durant gave him a close look. "Are you a game warden?"

"No. Why would you think so?"

With a half-smile, Durant said, "You're so nattily attired."

The ranger had the fleeting thought that he had done well to tie up his earflaps before coming into the camp. He said, "No, I'm not a game warden. I'm a ranger. It's by mere coincidence that I wear a shirt like the game wardens do. I drink coffee with them and sometimes play cards, but I'm a different breed of pup." Then he added, "My name is Ranger Redsleeves."

"I see." Durant's eyes roved up and down, back and forth, until he asked, "Have you shot much game with that saddle gun?"

"Not as much as some," replied the ranger. "I keep so busy advising people about the White Arrow code that I hardly have time to hunt for myself."

"Well," said Durant, glancing around his camp, "I think you'll find this camp well within your guidelines."

"By a few yards at least," agreed the ranger. "And now that I know you're aware of the regulation, I probably don't need to dwell on it."

Durant smiled. "It never hurts to remind the public. So many people are careless and have little respect for the law."

"It makes me glad to hear you say that." The man with the red sleeves turned to the horse, as if preparing to leave.

Durant's voice came to him. "But tell me, Ranger Two Rifles, what the fine is for violating the White Arrow."

The ranger turned back to face the other man. "I am Ranger Redsleeves," he said, as a little door opened in his mind and an arm waved a warning flag.

"Oh, excuse me. I thought you said Ranger Two Rifles."

"Quite all right," answered Redsleeves. "But you'll know the difference if you ever see him. He wears a cap like this, and a matching wool jacket—plaid, not a solid color like mine. And he wears pants of hunter green."

"That's quite a difference," said Durant.

"Yes," replied the ranger. "And he carries two rifles, of course."

"How silly of me to confuse you," said Durant, casting an earnest look from beneath the green bill of his cap.

"Think nothing of it," said Ranger Redsleeves. "But now, to answer your question, the fine varies. It is up to the judge and whether he thinks the offense was an honest mistake or a deliberate disregard for the rules."

Durant nodded.

"And your name, sir?" queried the ranger.

"Cook. Cameron's the first name, but I go by Cam."

"Very well, sir. It's been a pleasure to meet you." The ranger glanced at the sky. "I'd best be moving along."

"Don't let me keep you. And it's been a pleasure to meet you, Ranger—er, Redsleeves."

With a tip of the cap, the ranger mounted up and headed the horse out of camp. As he rode away, he heard the pickup door open and the radio station come on, followed by the sound of an axe thunking into a log.

Continuing in the same direction as the morning before, the rider of the dark horse now pondered what should be his next move. Quite evidently, the mastermind Daniel Durant was waiting for a prognostication of a quick drop in the temperature, and until such time, the head-hunting doctor would be waiting for a call. Thought the rider, if Durant is not listening to the radio later on, then perhaps he will have heard what he is listening for. The rider nodded to himself, or perhaps to his other self—the man in red nodding to the man in black.

Meanwhile the mud parade continued, as the frozen gumbo melted. The four wheelers, if possible, were muddier than the day before, and the passing pickups looked as if they had been engaged in a mud rally, which was for four-wheel-drive pickups what mud wrestling was for doyennes of the barroom.

Giving the road a wide berth, the rider continued at a leisurely pace until he approached the camp of the Old Scout. The first thing he noticed was that the Old Scout's pickup was in a different place. The second thing he noticed was that the mature gentleman was wearing a dove-grey felt hat, of the style much beloved by game wardens, western ranchers, and high-country outfitters. This hat matched well with the man's shirt, which was of a gentle pearl grey color, with the sleeves folded up at the wrists. The Old Scout's hands were bloody, for as his visitor noticed next, the venerable woodsman was skinning a cow elk. The animal hung upside down from the heavy branch of a stout pine tree, and the Old Scout was just beginning his task by skinning the hocks. The animal had already been field-dressed, which no doubt accounted for the red forearms of the Old Scout.

"Hello the camp," said Ranger Redsleeves.

"Hello to you, my young friend on the dark horse," said the older man, without turning around.

"What news?"

"I have shed the blood of the beast, and I am steeped in red up to my elbows, while you—" and here the Old Scout reached into the body cavity, pulled out a bloody drooping gob of yellow fat, and turned to face the visitor—"while you have undergone a bit of a change in color, also."

"Ranger Redsleeves," said that worthy, introducing himself.

"Well, mighty fine," replied the Old Scout. "And with a purpose, I'd suppose."

The ranger dismounted and said, in a low voice, "Quite so." For indeed, on the basis of the spiritual affinity he had felt with the Old Scout the day before, he had already decided to confide in him.

The man in grey gave a look of interest as he dropped the gob of fat. Then he made a tight half-smile, drew his bloody hand crossways in front of his mouth as if zipping his lips, and winked.

Whereupon the young man of the dark horse made a full disclosure of the case, which the older man listened to with grave attention as he skinned his elk.

At length the Old Scout paused from his work, shook his head, and said, "Microwave dinners. So much for dignity."

Then he gave his young friend a questioning look and asked, "Why do you think he was chopping wood?"

"To keep up a front, I suppose—and to be near the radio and the car phone."

The Old Scout nodded. "He mocks the things we love—the noble pursuit of hunting, the sanctity of human life, even the virtues of a natural diet." A shadow passed over the scout's face. "He would be the type, in other circumstances, to calumniate the light-featured members of the fair sex."

The young friend knitted his eyebrows in question.

"I mean, he holds humanity in such contempt that he would probably tell jokes about blondes."

"Oh," said the rider. He had heard such jokes and had found them mirthless.

"Well," said the Old Scout, with an air of gallantry, "count me in. If you need to send a messenger down to the ranger station, I'll be your Mercury. In my Cadillac, of course," he added, pointing with his bloody knife at the black pickup.

Ranger Redsleeves looked at the pickup, noted the "Stop Poaching" bumper sticker, and nodded. Then his attention was diverted by a vehicle stopping on the road.

Although its lower section was swathed in mud, the red Dodge truck was instantly recognizable—not only by its dual tires but also by its twin occupants.

"It's him!" cried a female voice, which was echoed by a shriek of delight and then followed by a grinding of gears. The red Dodge backed up a few yards and pulled into the Old Scout's camp. Both doors opened at once, and out of the cab came bounding the indomitable twin cowgirls.

Some readers may recall Wyoma and Wynema, the buxom blonde cowgirls from Chugwater, who had assisted the Ramrod Rider in his earlier encounter with Daniel Durant. Now here they were, vivacious as always, and he felt a blush creep into his face.

"Who are you this time?" asked Wyoma, hooking her right arm into his left.

"We knew we'd find you if we looked long enough," added Wynema, hooking the other arm.

"Ranger Redsleeves," said that same personage, not unaware that those red sleeves were now attached.

"Oh-h-h-h!" the girls said in unison, and, pressing against his red sleeves from both sides, they kissed him on the cheeks.

He felt the blush deepen, and then the cowgirls released him.

"You're so cute," said Wynema.

"And clever, too," said Wyoma. "I bet you catch him this time."

"Who's your friend?" asked Wynema.

"He looks like your uncle," added Wyoma.

"This is the Old Scout," said the spiritual nephew, turning to introduce his female friends to the denizen of the camp.

Introductions being made all around, the cowgirls were soon given to understand that discretion was of the essence.

"You bet . . ."

". . . mum's the word."

During this while, the Old Scout seemed to regain even more of his youthful spirit, for his green eyes sparkled as he exchanged pleasant conversation with his visitors. His young male visitor thought that a casual observer might never have guessed that this same Old Scout had been so saddened in his life—or, as that writer of memoirs would say, steeped in his own Byronic sorrows.

With his spirits thus rejuvenated, the Old Scout, having separated the elk from its hide and having washed the blood of the beast from his hands, proposed a round of refreshments. His guests accepting, he went into his tent and emerged with four camp chairs, and then with a second trip into the tent, he produced a half-gallon of orange juice and four camp cups—the latter of a speckled blue enamel, a style to be found in the best of camp outfits.

"No styrofoam in this camp," he said, with obvious pride, as he poured the beverage. Then holding his cup aloft, he said, "Let us drink to comradeship, and to the beauty of these two girls."

They drank.

The Old Scout raised his cup again. "Now let us toast the poetic quality of their names. There is singular beauty in an amphibrach." He smiled with avuncular warmth, and then, gazing off in the middle distance as his face softened with reminiscence, he said, "The first two women who left me, and the one who broke my heart after that, all had trochaic names. Perhaps, if love should bless my life one more time, it will do so with an amphibrach." He smiled again at the cowgirls. "You have brought happiness into my camp." He motioned with his cup. "Let us drink to youth, and beauty, and poetry."

They drank; then they sat in the camp chairs.

The Ramrod Rider (for thus he felt himself, despite the regalia of Ranger Redsleeves) was stirred by the sentiment of the moment. Nevertheless, he recalled the primacy of his mission. Lowering his empty cup to rest on his knee, he said, "I may need all of your help before this day is through." He looked at the cowgirls. "Are you planning to stay around?"

They looked at each other and then at him.

"We can stay right here . . ." said Wyoma.

" . . . and keep the Old Scout company," added Wynema.

"Well, mighty fine," said the host. "Fortunately, I laid in a good supply of granola bars, and I can fry up a mess of elk liver."

The cowgirls looked at one another with their nostrils flared in disgust.

"Or tenderloin steaks," amended the Old Scout.

The girls smiled.

"Sounds like you're all set," said the younger man. He rose from his chair. "I'll let you know by this evening, one way or the other." Then gathering the reins of the dark horse and taking his leave, he reluctantly departed the camp of the Old Scout and went back out into the muddy world, to resume the demeanor of Ranger Redsleeves.

Violation of the White Arrow—and the Ropes of Justice

On his way back to the pup tent, Ranger Redsleeves avoided casting long glances at the camp of Daniel Durant, but a few quick, furtive glances sufficed. Except for a light breeze rippling the blue tarp, the silver trailer and aqua-colored pickup sat in stillness. The doors of both vehicles were closed, the firewood was stacked neatly, and the axe was leaning against the woodpile. No sound came from the camp, except the familiar crackle of a plastic tarp in the wind. Perhaps the weather report came through, thought the rider of the dark horse.

Thinking of how he might beguile the next several hours, the rider decided to learn more of the country and to return, at intervals, to a vantage point from which he might observe any new activity in the neighborhood of the silver trailer.

This he did, until the western ridges began to cast their shadows once again, and the air began to chill noticeably. From an excellent high spot in back of the trailer, the watchful ranger could observe the camp as well as the road, and there he sat behind a screen of juniper while the dark horse dozed in a stand of aspens.

Presently the ranger's heart quickened as he saw a flash of blue and green, then the familiar V-shaped antenna amidst the other antennae. The vehicle disappeared and then reappeared as it sloshed along at a moderate rate of speed in the chocolate river of the forestry road. As expected, the sport utility vehicle turned into the camp below. The door of the vehicle opened, and the doctor stepped out. The door of the trailer opened, and the doctor stepped in. Then it was to horse and away for Ranger Redsleeves.

Good judgment prevailed as the rider elected to keep the dark horse down to a trot, thus to attract less attention. When he rode into the Old Scout's camp, therefore, it was not in a cloud of dust and a bath of horse sweat. Rather, he sauntered in, causing no immediate alarm with his trio of friends, who were seated in the camp chairs. They were eating jerky and drinking Budweiser in cans; a quick thought flashed that the Old Scout would be just the sort of man to recycle his aluminum.

"What's in the wind?" queried the Old Scout, who was seated between the two cowgirls.

"The doctor has arrived at Durant's trailer," said the rider, in a low but steady voice.

"Shall I summon the troops?" The Old Scout wiggled his beer can, as if to judge the amount therein.

"I think the time is ripe," said the young comrade, now stepping down from the horse and brushing a fleck of mud from his left sleeve.

The Old Scout tipped up his beer can, then lowered it and placed it in a plastic garbage bag, where it rattled against others. He smiled at his female guests. "Make yourselves at home," he said. "I'll be back to fry the steaks in a little while." Then he climbed into the cab of his pickup, fired up the engine, and drove away.

Wyoma and Wynema looked at Ranger Redsleeves.

"I think I'll ask you two girls to stand by," he said. "I have a hunch that if he makes a run for it, it'll be in this direction."

The girls stood up, following the example of the Old Scout as they emptied their beer cans and deposited them in the bag. Then they came to stand by Ranger Redsleeves, as before. Each of them hooking an arm into one of his, they pressed against him and planted a pair of kisses upon his blushing face. Notwithstanding the aroma of garlic and beer, it was not an entirely unpleasant sensation.

"That's for being a good ranger," said Wyoma.

"Out working while we sit in camp," added Wynema.

"Well," said Ranger Redsleeves, "thank you for your appreciation. I hope it won't be long now until we have our man. If you girls could just stand by, like I suggested, I'll go keep an eye on things."

"You bet," said the cowgirls, in unison.

Thereupon the ranger mounted up and rode out of the camp, turning once and looking back, and returning the wave of his two friends.

For his lookout at this time, Ranger Redsleeves chose a spot downstream, so to speak, of Durant's camp, so that if the fish slipped the first net, the red-sleeved angler would be at the ready. From this spot, which was about forty yards off the road, he had a clear view of the camp and of the road beyond, from which direction the official vehicles would come.

After about twenty minutes, during which time various vehicles had passed in each direction, the ranger saw a four-wheeler turn off the road and head his way. As the vehicle came closer, the vigilant ranger perceived that the machine carried two people—the bearded hunter from the morning before, and his open-mouthed apprentice. The young man had his rifle attached with the sling across his chest, making an "X" with the bandoleer, while his mentor presumably had his weapon secured in the molded plastic gun case mounted on the front rack of the vehicle.

The bearded man brought the four-wheeler to a stop and turned off the engine. "Seen anything?"

The ranger shook his head, hoping to imply that he didn't wish to speak—a tactic sometimes employed by elk hunters to discourage others from spooking the quarry.

"Man from Rawlins saw two spike runnin' together, right on the other side of the ridge behind ya. Two guys from Cheyenne said they saw a four-point walk right across the road in front of 'em, an' all they had was cow permits." The man shook his head back and forth and made a spluttering sound with his lips, then spoke again. "This fella that drives up each day from Saratoga says there was a big herd spotted over on Troublesome."

The ranger remained silent.

"There's a camp of six hunters from Arkansaw, and they got a cow and a calf hung up in their camp." He turned to his young companion. "Muddy mess of meat, ain't it, boy?"

The young hunter nodded without closing his mouth.

"Well," said the older man, "we'd ought to be movin' along." He pushed a button, and the engine churned into action. Then the man spoke above the noise of the engine. "There's two pair o' tracks right down by the road here, which I want to show this boy. Good visitin' with ya."

The ranger nodded.

The man let out the clutch, and with a mild lurch, the vehicle was on its way, leaving ruts in the soft ground as it made a semi-circle and headed back to the road. The two passengers bounced up and down as the four-wheeler crossed the road;

then the machine stopped and became quiet, and the two hunters dismounted.

The older man was speaking, but the words themselves were not discernible at the distance. Apparently for the apprentice's edification, the master was pointing at the ground as he spoke. Then he put his hands up by his hat brim, with the fingers spread out and pointing upward, in simulation of antlers. The tip of the rifle wiggled as the young man nodded. The duo followed the trail a few more steps.

Suddenly the ranger's attention was diverted by the approach of a convoy. The vehicles were of various colors, denoting various agencies, but they all had blue and red lights flashing as they positioned themselves between the road and the camp.

Two men in uniform got out of a green four-wheel-drive passenger vehicle and walked up to the trailer door. At that moment, another door opened beneath the dark recesses of the blue awning, and a fugitive in military camouflage went bounding into a clump of brush. When the figure emerged from the brush, Ranger Redsleeves saw clearly that it was Daniel Durant, wearing the green cap.

With a touch of the rider's heels, the dark horse was in motion. The rider was wondering whether to pull the Winchester, when he saw Durant head for the abandoned four-wheeler. In an instant, the large but agile man was aboard the device and had it moving.

The chase was on. The red-clad rider kept the horse away from the treacherously muddy road, and then from the corner of his eye he saw a black pickup—that of the Old Scout, who would have been in the rear of the convoy and who was now pursuing, now overtaking, and now passing the fugitive, who gave way to the larger vehicle.

A hundred yards ahead, the black pickup slid sideways and came to a halt, forming a roadblock. The man on the four-wheeler, who had seemed to be in the process of opening the gun case, now put both hands on the handlebars and veered sharply off the road to the right, and through the timber.

The dark horse cleared the road in two bounds and plunged into the timber behind the whining four-wheeler. The machine was headed in the general direction of the Old Scout's camp and would probably pass behind it.

The engine subsided and then accelerated, and the pursuing rider saw the four-wheeler go up and over a mounded dirt barricade.

Daniel Durant had just committed a flagrant violation of the White Arrow code, and all it stood for.

The dark horse followed, and as horse and rider cleared the mound of dirt, the four-wheeler could be seen weaving through the timber, not a hundred yards ahead. Suddenly in its pathway stepped two people, blonde persons of a curvaceous appearance.

Rather than swerve or slow down, the vehicle accelerated, and as the girls stepped to each side, they twirled their ropes.

From the distance, it was difficult to distinguish Wyoma from Wynema, but suffice it to say that the girl on the left made the first throw. The loop settled around the shoulders of the driver, who seemed to have a good grip on the machine, for his momentum jerked the girl forward—until her roping partner sailed a second loop and made a good catch. With the two of them digging their heels into the ground, they brought the fugitive tumbling backwards off the vehicle and onto the soft earth, where the Fidel Castro cap rolled to the side. The four-wheeler continued forward for another ten yards until it came up against a tree, where it sputtered and died.

By the time the red-sleeved ranger arrived, Wynema had put three wraps and a hooey around Durant's ankles, and Wyoma had put a couple of more wraps around his arms as he tried to sit up. The would-be fugitive looked like a large, pale-headed, green fish in a net.

Thus did the twin cowgirls from Chugwater, in league with their brave comrades young and older, help the cause of justice in the high country of Wyoming.

* * * * *

Later that evening, once again in the black garments of his calling, the Ramrod Rider packed up his meager camp. Before returning to the ranger station, he passed by the camp of the Old Scout, there to take leave.

That gentleman was in the process of pouring hot chocolate into the cups of Wyoma and Wynema, who were seated by the campfire, snug in their matching sheepskin coats. All three people looked up at the approach of the Ramrod Rider.

"Well," said the rider, "I guess my work is done—for now, at least."

"Yes," replied the Old Scout, returning the pan of hot chocolate to the camp stove and picking up a bottle of peppermint schnapps. "Now it's a matter of how deep his pockets are, and what kind of lawyers he can get."

"At least we caught him," said Wynema.

"Puss and Puncher will be so glad," Wyoma added.

"True," said the Ramrod Rider. "We've done our best, and we've closed things out for the time being." He shook his head. "Until he's back on the street again, there's plenty more just like him, though. And so I've got to move on."

A tinge of sadness hung in the air, until Wyoma said, "But we know you'll be back."

"You can't stay away forever," said Wynema.

"These girls are right," said the Old Scout. "And when you come back, you know you can always hang your hat at my place." He stepped forward and grasped the younger man's hand in a firm handshake, as his green eyes sparkled in the firelight.

The Ramrod Rider felt his eyes begin to mist, and he might even have given way to unmanly emotion, until he saw a sight that relieved all sadness. For there, as he looked beyond the Old Scout at the two young ladies seated in their chairs, with their blonde hair shining in the amber glow of the campfire, he saw that they had their lips pursed in a playful double smile; and then two eyelids dropped in a double wink for the Ramrod Rider.

About the Author

John D. Nesbitt lives in the plains country of Wyoming, where he teaches English and Spanish at Eastern Wyoming College. His articles, reviews, fiction, and poetry have appeared in numerous magazines and anthologies. He has had more than thirty books published, including short story collections, contemporary novels, and traditional westerns, as well as textbooks for his courses. John has won many awards for his work, including two awards from the Wyoming State Historical Society (for fiction), two awards from Wyoming Writers for encouragement of other writers and service to the organization, two Wyoming Arts Council literary fellowships (one for fiction, one for non-fiction), a Will Rogers Medallion Award for *Dark Prairie* (a frontier mystery) and another for *Thorns on the Rose* (a poetry collection), a Western Writers of America Spur finalist award for his novel *Raven Springs*, and the Spur award itself for his short story "At the End of the Orchard" and for his novels *Trouble at the Redstone* and *Stranger in Thunder Basin*. His recent work includes *Poacher's Moon,* a contemporary novel; *Blue Horse Mesa*, a collection of western stories; and *Field Work*, a retro-noir fiction collection. Visit his website at www.johndnesbitt.com

John D. Nesbitt

ANTELOPE SKY

STORIES OF THE MODERN WEST

"NESBITT IS A TRUE ARTIST."
—WESTERN AMERICAN LITERATURE

Published by SpeakingVolumes

Visit us at www.speakingvolumes.us

John D. Nesbitt

SEASONS IN THE FIELDS

STORIES OF A GOLDEN WEST

"NESBITT IS A TRUE ARTIST."
—WESTERN AMERICAN LITERATURE

Published by SpeakingVolumes

Visit us at www.speakingvolumes.us

John D. Nesbitt

WEST OF ROCK RIVER

"NESBITT IS A TRUE ARTIST."
—WESTERN AMERICAN LITERATURE

Published by SpeakingVolumes

Visit us at www.speakingvolumes.us

John D. Nesbitt

NORTH OF CHEYENNE

"NESBITT IS A TRUE ARTIST."
—WESTERN AMERICAN LITERATURE

Published by SpeakingVolumes

Visit us at www.speakingvolumes.us

John D. Nesbitt

MAN FROM
WOLF RIVER

"NESBITT IS A TRUE ARTIST."
—WESTERN AMERICAN LITERATURE

Published by SpeakingVolumes

Visit us at www.speakingvolumes.us

John D. Nesbitt

NOT A RUSTLER

"NESBITT IS A TRUE ARTIST."
—WESTERN AMERICAN LITERATURE

Published by SpeakingVolumes

Visit us at www.speakingvolumes.us

www.ingramcontent.com/pod-product-compliance
Lightning Source LLC
Chambersburg PA
CBHW032040240626
47154CB00003B/1000